BOOK ONE – THE TATTOOED GIRL SERIES

JESSICA PENOT

www.jessicapenot.com

Published Internationally by Jessica Penot
Copyright © 2018 Jessica Penot

Exclusive cover © 2018 Fiona Jayde Media Designs
Interior design by Tamara Cribley www.deliberatepage.com

PRINT ISBN
978-1-7326928-1-7
EBOOK ISBN
978-1-7326928-0-0

Editor - Joanna D'Angelo
Copy Editor - Brenda Heald

I dedicate this book to all my clients and all the people that feel alone. It is a terrible thing to feel like you don't belong and I believe there is always a special magic for those who feel unloved.

ACKNOWLEDGMENTS

I would like to thank Joanna D'Angelo for pushing me to finish this book and keeping me writing even when I wanted to give up. She is a wonderful editor and a wonderful coach.

ALSO AVAILABLE

The Accidental Witch Series:
Book 1 The Accidental Witch
Book 2 The Darkest Art

Single Titles:
Circe
Death's Dream Kingdom

Twilight Saint Series:
The Twilight Saint

Haunting Series:
Haunted Chattanooga
Haunted North Alabama

CHAPTER 1

The oldest and strongest emotion of mankind is fear, and the oldest and strongest kind of fear is fear of the unknown.

~ H. P. Lovecraft

I WAS ALWAYS COLD IN the morning. Even in the spring, I felt like my skin turned to ice while I slept. I crawled out of bed and hopped into the shower. I stayed under the warm curtain of water as long as I could and then I forced my wet body back out into the cold.

I could always see my past when I was naked. It was etched on me in long scars and ink. I didn't remember much of my early childhood, but I didn't need to. When I stepped out of the shower, I glanced over my shoulder at my image in the mirror and shuddered. My entire back was covered in an enormous tattoo that had been there for as long as I could remember. It was a reminder of what I was: an abandoned girl with parents who had used her as a template for their madness. I had to twist my neck to see it in the mirror. I never let anyone else look at it, but it seemed to me that it had changed and grown with time. When I was a little girl, it had just been a door. Now, it was intricate. It was a door into a hillside, and it was wrapped in ivy and flowers. A brook flowed beside the door. It was in color. I loathed the thing, so I looked away. I tried to pretend it wasn't real.

I didn't just pretend the tattoo wasn't real. I pretended most of my life was different. I pretended I hadn't bounced from one foster home to another. I pretended that, at sixteen, I wasn't essentially living on my own. I closed my eyes and envisioned that somewhere out there I had a loving mother and father and that I was an average teenager. All my life, I had worked twice as hard as everyone else to maintain this façade. I always got straight As in school. I had been advanced two grades. I wore boring clothes and tried to blend in so no one would know that, underneath it all, I was an aberration.

I had been through three foster homes since I was abandoned in an emergency room at the age of four. I tried not to think about my first foster homes, but I did remember the emergency room. I remembered waking up and everyone staring at me like I was from outer space. I was naked. My name had been written across my forehead in Sharpie: *Jane.* Across my chest were the words: *Love is the gateway that will set the old ones free.* And, of course, on my back was that massive tattoo. My parents might as well have written, "Circus Freak. Handle with Care." on my arms.

It was May and it should have been much warmer, but winter had lingered. It clung to the air like an old ghost. I covered my tattoo in heavy sweaters and tried to keep it covered. I never wore bathing suits or tank tops. I hid under big clothes. I was lucky it was still cold because I would have been miserable if it had been hot.

I took the bus to school. I sat in the back and tried to avoid notice. This was easy enough. Most of the other kids were well practiced at ignoring me. I was a shadow to them. I wasn't even important enough to bully or mock anymore. When I was young, I hadn't been as good at hiding and the kids had been ruthless, but I had become an expert at making myself completely forgettable. I was nothing. I knew this should have made me sad. It should have filled me with woe, but I had my books. The laughing girls around me seemed far away compared to the characters in my stories.

I had one friend. Helen Yee. Helen was my opposite. Her features were a mixture of Asian and white. She had short black hair and eyes the color of the sky at twilight. The color lived somewhere between the blue of day and the black of night. She was small and curvy, with a shape I imagined would make boys look at her with lust. Her fair skin and blue eyes were disarming when mixed with her Asian features so that she had an otherworldly quality that could be described as haunting. She dressed however she pleased and, most of the time, whatever she was wearing was a little bit shocking. She would wear striped witch stockings from a Halloween costume with pleated shorts, and a man's shirt with a bow tie or combat boots with what looked like a bridesmaid's dress from 1972 that she'd dug out of the trash. She didn't care what anyone thought of her. She was quick-witted and fierce, and I loved everything about her that was different from me. She was three years older than me, but she didn't treat me like a kid. She started kindergarten a year late, she said, because she'd moved around so much when she was a little kid. She was nineteen and I was sixteen and she always seemed to have all the wisdom I wished I had. When Helen was around, she made all the girls that ignored me seem like pale shadows.

"Are you ready?" Helen asked after school. We sat together on my bed, plotting. Helen had drawn a large picture of an eyeball on the back of her arm. It was so bright and vibrant that I would have thought it was a real tattoo if I hadn't known Helen's penchant for self-illustration. Helen was the only one who knew about my back tattoo. She thought it was a gift and told me to show it off, but I wasn't brave like Helen.

"Just another house," I muttered. "It isn't like staying with Mrs. Blankenship has been a joy. Getting out will be good."

"You have to be a little excited. You're graduating two years early. You're going to college. You have a full scholarship. You'll be free."

I shrugged. I tried not to think about the future. It was a dark tunnel to nowhere. The only reason I was able to graduate early and go to college was because my foster mother, Mrs. Blankenship, went along with it. She collected her government check and deposited it, and said she'd keep her mouth shut about me going away to college at the ripe young age of sixteen. Even though she treated me with polite indifference, she had given me a home for almost ten years and kept me from being tossed back into the foster care system. She lied to my caseworker and I helped her lie because I didn't want to go to another foster home. Mrs. Blankenship's lies kept me safe. I lived in constant terror that my caseworker would figure out how unsupervised I was and shuffle me into yet another nightmare. I wouldn't go to college. I would be stuck repeating high school because I wasn't a teen or even a person; I was a number in a system that didn't account for individual differences.

"We are going to college. And we'll be living in a castle. You are done with foster care. Aren't you a little bit excited?" Helen asked me.

I rolled my eyes. "We're going to be killed and eaten by some crazy serial killer."

"You read too many books."

"You don't read enough books."

"Don't worry so much. It's a good job with room and board included. In a castle. Can you believe it? We're going to live in a castle and go to college together. It doesn't get any better than that."

"That's what makes it so creepy," I said. "It's too good to be true. Getting paid to stay someplace at night? Who pays someone to stay in a house at night? No one does that. Oh wait, I know who does that. Serial killers. We're going to be killed and turned into a floral arrangement in some psycho killer's basement or even worse… CPS is going to find me and put me back into foster care."

Helen sighed. "Mrs. Blankenship will cover for you. She wants her money, so she won't tell anyone you've left.

You'll be fine. And I promise you that Edward is not a serial killer. He's a nice guy who needs someone to keep an eye on his grandmother at night. It's the perfect job."

CH⋀PTER 2

*Who knows the end? What has risen may
sink, and what has sunk may rise.*

~ H.P. Lovecraft

HELEN AND I LEFT THE day after graduation. We
weren't starting college until fall, but we had jobs and I had
no desire to stay at home a moment longer than I had to.
Neither of us was leaving anything behind that we'd miss,
so we were both eager to get on the road. We drove both to
escape everything that had happened before and to move
on to a more hopeful future. Mrs. Blankenship was sitting
by the window as I dragged my two heavy bags toward the
door. She stared blankly out into the backyard. There was a
cigarette in her hand. It had gone out, but she didn't notice.

I was sixteen. I felt entirely on my own. And I was terrified. In truth, I had been on my own since Mr. Blankenship
died. Since then, it was like Mrs. Blankenship had died,
too. She rarely left her room and spent more time crying
than working. She hadn't done any of the things that a
mom was supposed to do for her child. I'd been working

part-time and buying my own clothes for as long as I could remember. I even cooked our meals and cleaned the house. I didn't know what she would do after I left. I hoped she would be okay.

I threw my bags in the back of my rusty old Jeep. I rarely drove the thing because I couldn't afford the gas, but I had just enough in the tank to get Helen and me to campus. I waved goodbye to Mrs. Blankenship and wondered if I'd ever see her again. I knew that the thought was somewhat irrational, but I felt sad at the idea and the feeling lingered. Mrs. Blankenship had never been loving or affectionate, but she'd never been abusive either. She was never present, but at least she'd always been there. She was my almost-mother. Leaving her felt like I was severing all ties to my childhood. What little childhood I'd had. And yet, I was only sixteen. I felt both too young and too old at the same time.

I looked over at Helen. She was all smiles. She put on some music. I never fully understood Helen's music. It was loud and incoherent, but I was sure it was cool in a way I could never comprehend. I never really knew why Helen wanted to hang out with me. Helen was cool. I was sure of that. She was pretty and well-shaped, and she wore clothes that whispered of something dangerous and bold. Yet, she was always around me for some unknown reason. I never saw her with anyone else. It was like I was the only person that existed to her. She had a boyfriend, but I had never met him. I never saw her with anyone else. Everyone else in her life seemed distant, like a memory or an old photograph.

This is what bothered me the most about Helen. I never met her boyfriend Jake. He was an enigma that took her away from me for long stretches of time. She would disappear for weeks to be with him. It made me wonder. We were best friends, so why didn't she introduce me to her boyfriend? Why didn't she introduce me to anyone?

I sat down and I put my foot on the gas in a way that made the Jeep take off at something that resembled warp speed. I drove so rarely; it was nice to feel the wind in my hair when I did.

"Woo hoo!" Helen yelled as I drove. "I thought we would never get away from this hell hole."

My smile didn't quite mirror her exuberant grin, but a feeling was beginning to unfurl inside me. I didn't know what it was yet, but it sure felt good.

"So long Craphole!" Helen's bracelets clanged together as she made an obscene gesture out the window toward our tiny town. Her thin arm was disturbingly graceful while it moved.

Sometimes I found myself wishing I possessed half the beauty and grace my friend did. I was chronically jealous of her straight black hair and her striking blue eyes. I wanted to look like Helen so badly. I had curly, brown hair and dark eyes. My skin was too dark to make me white and too light for me to be black. Or so the kids at school had told me. I'd been teased for my strange appearance as a child. Especially because of the freckles on my face. The kids called me "freak girl" because I didn't know who my parents were. So, therefore, I had no idea what my ethnicity was, but I had to assume it was mixed. I always wanted to be Asian like Helen because she was the most beautiful girl I had ever known. When I was in public, I tried my hardest to not stand out because people always asked me what I was. And I could never tell them because I didn't know.

I hid beneath baggy clothes. Not just because of my tattoo, but also because I was tall and too thin, and my hair was long and big and curly. I generally kept my hair in one thick braid down my back. My clothes came from the Goodwill, but they lacked the style and creativity of Helen's outfits. Besides, I was more concerned with making sure my tattoo was covered at all times to worry about style. Mostly, I wore jeans and long-sleeved shirts and tried to forget I had a freak stamp on my back.

The sun was setting as we sped along the highway. The pink and purple of the vanishing sun painted the sky with an uncommon beauty. I basked in that light. Maybe everything would be good from now on. I was hopeful.

CH⋀PTER 3

Terror made me cruel.

~ Emily Brontë

HELEN WAS QUIET FOR MUCH of the drive. I knew that this was definitely a sign that she had something important to say. Helen could talk for hours about nothing, but when she had something significant to talk about, she became mute. I didn't press for conversation. I was content just having her beside me as I drove.

Huntington College was a small school in a small town. The road from our hometown of Gateshead, Massachusetts, to Huntington, Virginia, wove through the Appalachian Mountains. It was lined with large, old-growth trees that had watched, in silent majesty, the birth of our nation and the unfolding history of the South.

Suddenly, Helen blurted out what she'd been holding in. "My boyfriend says I can stay with him in his apartment." The guilt washed over her face in a deep crimson wave.

"Oh." It was all I could say. I felt numb. I knew I should feel something, but it was like all my emotional responses vanished. Helen did things like this all the time. I would be the center of her world and then I would ask her to come to a movie with me and she would stand me up. She would spend hours with me in my room talking and then disappear for a week. I had the flu once and she sat by my bed for the entire week and when I woke up, I couldn't find her. Helen was capricious and I should have seen this coming.

"I know I should stay with you at Thornfield and I don't want to leave you with some crazy serial killer, but you know Jake is really important to me and he really wants me to live with him. He's in love with me and wants us to be together forever. Isn't that romantic?" Helen said in a rush.

I put my hand on Helen's arm. "That's wonderful. Truly." I meant it. I wanted Helen to be happy. I would be fine. I was used to being on my own, in any case. "Don't worry," I said. "I'm sure the owner isn't a serial killer. I'll be fine. I'm glad I have a job and a place to live."

"Why are you always so nice?" Helen seemed even more frustrated. "It just makes things worse. Here I am dumping you at the last second before you we even get there."

"I will be fine. I have survived worse."

Helen looked even more guilty and turned even redder. She looked like she was going to cry. She pulled at the spiked dog collar she wore around her neck and shifted in her seat. "I am so sorry."

I didn't want to make her feel worse, although she couldn't quite suppress her excitement over moving in with her boyfriend.

"Do you think it'll be a problem that you won't be living there? Don't they need an adult? I'm only sixteen."

"They think you're an adult. I filled out your application and sent in a fake ID."

"You lied? You sent in a fake ID? I'm not comfortable with that. What about the car? How will you get back and forth to school without my help and how will I afford gas without your help?"

"Don't worry about me. I can take care of myself. You won't need gas money, either. You'll be able to walk to class. The house was built by the founder of the Huntington College. It's practically on campus, it's so close."

I stuffed down my anxiety. I should count my blessings. I had no money and no family and a friend who loved me enough to make sure I had room and board, so I could go to school. If it weren't for Helen, I wouldn't even be going to college. I had received scholarships to a number of schools, but without money for room and board, I wouldn't have gone anywhere. Helen had found me a job that made it possible for me to follow my dreams. If it weren't for Helen, I would be stuck with Mrs. Blankenship, or worse, I would be still stuck in high school and working part-time until I was eighteen and legally old enough to go off on my own.

I smiled at my friend. "Thank you, Helen. I don't know what I would do without you. I couldn't have done any of this without you."

"Shut up!" Helen yelled. "I told you that you being this nice is only making it harder on me. I'm abandoning you with some crazy old lady and her weird grandson. You should hate me right now."

I only laughed. "You got me a job and a place to live. How can I hate you?"

Helen smiled. "Fine. Don't hate me, but at least let me stay the first night with you and get you settled in. You're the best friend I've ever had. I don't want you thinking that I'm the type of friend who'd just dump you for some guy."

"I know you aren't. You're a loyal friend," I told her. It was true that we both had tough childhoods, although Helen didn't say much about hers. I didn't pry, either. I knew what it was to have secrets like the big old secret on my back. Neither of us had come from families that made it easy. We both had to do what was necessary to get by. Which was why Helen's announcement really was amazing. At least one of us had a happily ever after. Or at least, a happy for now."

"I *do* love Jake, you know. I'm not just doing what I have to do. I really want to be with him."

I smiled brightly. I knew that. Helen and Jake had been together since my first year in high school. Jake was the reason Helen was going to Huntington College. Helen wanted to be a doctor. She was super smart and had been offered scholarships at every university in the state, better schools with better pre-med programs. She could have gone anywhere and done anything, but she'd chosen Jake. Of course, I wanted to be with Helen, too, and I wanted to be a doctor, just like Helen, so I'd chosen Huntington for the same reason. I wanted to be near my only friend and

Huntington had offered me a very generous scholarship. Helen was the guiding light in my life and she always seemed to be helping me make the right decisions and taking care of me. Like a guardian angel, except she was here, in person.

The car slowed down and I caught my first glimpse of Huntington. It was a small town nestled in the mountains and it had the quiet charm of an English village, or what I imagined an English village would look like. Out of time. The buildings looked like they were built in the late 1800s and they gave the town a charm that most modern cities lacked. The main street was bustling with life. People were hurrying along the sidewalk, sitting in cafes, or going in and out of the various shops and businesses that lined the thoroughfare. Everyone seemed to have a clear purpose. I wanted that, too.

We drove through the downtown and onto Huntington's campus. I took a deep breath. The campus looked like something out of a classic novel. The sunlight hit the limestone and cast strange shadows on the old buildings. The campus was built in a neo-gothic style and all the buildings really did look like English manor houses. Beautiful, but a little intimidating.

We drove through the campus until we came to the very edge of the school grounds and stopped at a large black gate. Helen got out and opened it for us. We drove down a short road and up to a house that was so beautiful, it left me breathless. It really was a castle. The kind of place that a Jane Austen heroine would live, after she married the hero.

I knew that Helen was talking. I could hear her voice, but I couldn't understand anything she was saying. The only thing I could see or feel or hear was the house. Thornfield Hall.

I stepped out of the car onto the cobblestone driveway. Gazing at the stone façade of the mansion, my heart pounded in my chest like an old bass drum. My breathing quickened. And I felt a tingling that turned into a burning sensation up and down my back. My tattoo. I didn't know why it was bothering me all of a sudden. I'd had it my entire life, so it couldn't be an infection. Maybe all the stress of the past few weeks was getting to me. Almost as soon as the burning feeling had begun it stopped. I sighed with relief. I certainly didn't need to get sick before I even started my new job.

I took a step closer to the place that would be my home for the next four years. It was sprawling. It was intimidating. It was unlike anything I had ever seen. I loved it.

Thornfield was all gray. Dark, smoky gray stones made up the façade of the huge home. And the roof was a darker, charcoal gray. I counted at least ten windows on the second floor, but there were probably more on the other side too. Who knew how many bedrooms were in it? The windows had a lattice crisscross design. I knew that because the richest kid in my hometown had a house with lattice windows. I remember looking it up at the library when I was younger. I couldn't wait to stand at my bedroom window and see the world through the little squares. The grounds surrounding the home were beautiful, too. There were so many trees on the property, it was like Thornfield had been built in the middle of a forest. Thornfield was perfect. Just perfect.

Helen punched me gently on the arm and pulled me out of my trance. "What's wrong with you?"

"Nothing," I said, shaking my head. "It's just so beautiful."

Helen shook her head. "I guess. It looks kind of creepy to me. Remember that old movie, *The Haunting of Hillhouse?* It looks just like Hillhouse. I don't know how we are going to sleep in there. You know, if you can't go through with this, you can crash with Jake and me until you find another job. We'll take care of you until you find something."

"No," I whispered. "This is perfect."

"Are you sure?" Helen asked again. She sounded worried and relieved at the same time.

I only nodded. I'd never been so sure of anything in my life. I'd never felt like I belonged anywhere. But Thornfield Hall felt like home. Helen and I grabbed our bags and we walked up to the front door and rang the doorbell. The bell echoed through the massive house. A petite woman, in a dark green sweater and a pleated gray skirt, answered the door. The woman looked like she was in her mid-fifties. She had friendly blue eyes and short blonde hair that was turning gray. She looked maternal and friendly. She reminded me of Julie Andrews from those old movies with nice English governesses where they sang pretty songs. She smiled brightly.

"You must be Miss Jane Marsh." the woman said. She reached out and shook my hand, ignoring Helen entirely. Maybe it was Helen's outrageous outfit and the dog collar she wore around her neck? Or maybe it was because I was tall and seemed older, and Helen was short?

"Yes," I said with a shy smile.

The woman beamed as she opened the door wide and welcomed us in.

"Wonderful! I'm so glad you made it. I'm Mrs. Fairfax, the housekeeper. Come in, come in."

My eyes almost popped out as Mrs. Fairfax led us through the massive foyer. The floor was made of marble so shiny I could see my reflection. The marble staircase marched up to the second-floor landing, which was essentially a balcony that stretched around the interior of the house and branched off into two long hallways. Not to be outdone by the elegant floor, an ornate chandelier hung high above our heads. I almost got whiplash craning my neck back as I counted the tiers. It looked like a crystal wedding cake.

Mrs. Fairfax ushered us into a sitting room off the foyer. The floor was covered in oriental rugs and bookshelves lined the walls from floor to ceiling. A large stained-glass window, depicting a woman in a red gown, illuminated the room in a strange, red-tinted glow. I blinked a few times to adjust my eyes to the red room.

"I'm so glad you're here!" Mrs. Fairfax exclaimed. "It is so hard to get help here at night, with all the rumors, you know. I'm thrilled to have found you."

"Rumors?" I asked.

"Oh dear," Mrs. Fairfax said, raising her eyebrows. "You don't know about the rumors? I thought I was very clear about them in my emails."

I glanced at Helen who looked guilty, again. She was keeping a lot of secrets about this job. "Sorry about that," Helen whispered to me. "I didn't pass that email along to you. I forgot. You're not superstitious in any case."

Mrs. Fairfax sighed, as though she had told this story many times. "The local lore says that this house is haunted—"

"I don't believe in ghosts," I interrupted.

"Well," Mrs. Fairfax said softly, "I am glad to hear that, at least." She smiled "Nevertheless," she continued, "the rumors are terrible. They say that Mr. Rochester's wife haunts Thornfield."

"Mr. Rochester was married?" I guess he must have been older than I'd thought."

"Richard Rochester." Mrs. Fairfax raised her thin arched brows. He was the Great-Great-Great Grandfather of Edward, the current owner of Thornfield Hall and the sole heir of the Rochester fortune. The company is called The Rochester Group and they own properties all over the world, including Huntington. Richard Rochester was the founder of Huntington College. He built this college in the grand tradition of Oxford and Cambridge." She heaved a deep sigh. "The rumors of the hauntings have been around for years, although I have never seen one inkling of anything ghostly in this grand home."

"I could never be scared off by a ghost story," I said confidently.

"Well, I am very pleased to hear that. Edward will be thrilled that we have someone to stay at night. I feel that you should have read the emails I sent you explaining the house's history, however; that is a critical factor in the job. It isn't good that you disregarded it."

"Oh," I said. I was quick on my feet and made up a cover story. I couldn't believe Helen had told me so little about the job. "I am just really tired. I am sorry. I just drove eight hours and my mind is mush. I'm not normally this forgetful. Of course, I read the emails. I just don't worry too much about superstition and ghost stories."

"I am sorry," Mrs. Fairfax answered with concern. "I forgot how long you've been driving. Do you need a drink or to use the bathroom?"

"No," I shook my head. "I'm fine. This place is so beautiful. I've never seen anything like it. I imagine its history is fascinating."

"Indeed it is." Mrs. Fairfax smiled. "The Rochester family founded this town in 1847. The Rochesters are a very old English aristocratic family. Richard Rochester's father was the fifth Earl of Huntington. They shipped the entire house, brick-by-brick, from their family lands in Northumbria. Adele is Edward's grandmother. Edward is going to *Yale*," she said, leaning in as though confiding a terrible secret. "Quite shocking at first, mind you. But we are getting used to it." Mrs. Fairfax shook her head as though she was still having some trouble adjusting to that fact.

I was relieved to know that my employer was looking out for his grandmother and wasn't some creepy guy who just wanted a young woman living in his house with him.

When Helen described the job, I thought I was going to be spending a lot more time alone with a strange man. I felt like a weight had been lifted from my shoulders. I would primarily be working for Mrs. Fairfax and Edward would be gone at Yale. I might not have to meet him at all. Helen had made it sound like he would be creeping in and out all night. Okay, I really needed to stop listening to Helen. I loved Helen, but her narratives confused me. One minute she was telling me we were going to be living alone with a strange man and his grandmother and the next she was telling me he wasn't a serial killer and the next I found out everything was completely different. I tried not think about it. I tried not to think about Edward. On the other hand, I couldn't help but be curious about him. Why would the great-great-great grandson of the founder of Huntington College go to Yale?

"You look tired," Mrs. Fairfax commented. "I should show you to your room and let you get settled in. We can talk more after you've rested."

We followed Mrs. Fairfax through Thornfield Hall. Every room we walked past only served to convince me that I had somehow drifted out of real life and into a dream. I peeked into a huge room with vaulted ceilings that had to be the library. The walls were lined with bookshelves so high that there was a balcony halfway up that stretched around its entire interior. There was also a spiral staircase at both ends and ladders placed strategically throughout. You could fit three of my town's libraries in Thornfield's. I couldn't wait to explore it.

The long halls resembled an art gallery: landscapes of dark castles, wind-swept cliffs, and stormy forests contrasted with portraits of beautiful and mysterious women in jewel-toned gowns and dangerously handsome men. I wanted to stop and linger, but I could only peek into rooms as we passed them. I saw a music room with an enormous grand piano and another sitting room with a cozy-looking fireplace. There were numerous bedrooms with huge beds and lavish décor. There was more, so much more, but any further explorations would have to wait until I was settled.

By the time we arrived at my room, my head was spinning. Mrs. Fairfax opened the door and I couldn't help but gasp. The bedroom was bigger than Mrs. Blankenship's entire house. The huge canopy bed had dark red toile bed curtains. At the far end of the room, a stone fireplace had a cheery fire in full bloom. Two large floral upholstered chairs, which could fit two people each, sat facing the fire. A rose-wood dresser and matching desk were ensconced in one corner, but the best part had to be the huge picture window that took up an entire wall. It faced out onto an Olympic-sized swimming pool. I didn't even know how to swim. I'd always been too terrified of anyone seeing my tattoo to dare put on a swimming suit.

Beyond the pool, I could see riding stables. There were horses grazing in the tall grass. I'd never ridden a horse either, although every romance novel I'd ever read always had a heroine who loved horses and riding.

"I'm sorry it is so small," Mrs. Fairfax said. "We keep most of the house closed now. The larger rooms are so hard to maintain. This room has a nice view and it is right next to Miss Adele's room, so it will make her feel safe knowing you are here. Here's the bathroom." Mrs. Fairfax opened a door revealing a gleaming bathroom with ultra-modern fixtures, a large marble shower with a rain-shower head and a special bath-tub, that looked like it had been tailor-made for an old woman with mobility issues. "I hope you don't mind sharing a bathroom with Miss Adele?"

"Not at all," I said.

"Dinner is at six in the kitchen. We don't use the dining room when Edward isn't here. It just doesn't seem right," Mrs. Fairfax said. She wandered out of the room before we had time to respond.

"We're getting out of here," Helen said. "Grab your stuff. Don't worry about anything. I'm taking care of you."

CH▲PTER 4

The human heart has hidden treasures. In secret kept, in silence sealed; The thoughts, the hopes, the dreams, the pleasures, Whose charms are broken if revealed.

~ Charlotte Brontë

"WHAT?" I WAS HARDLY EVEN paying attention to Helen. I had almost forgotten she was there. I was so lost in the details of a large embroidered tapestry hanging on the wall above the bed that I hadn't heard her desperate tone.

"Grab your stuff. This place is weird. It's like some old mausoleum. Definitely a thirty-five out of ten on the creepy-meter and I'm not leaving you here. Let's ditch this place before anyone notices."

"I love it," I said.

"Are you crazy? Mrs. Fairfax seems a few eggs short of a dozen and this place fell out of an old horror movie. This place is haunted as hell and I don't think it is the good kind of haunted either."

"I think Mrs. Fairfax seems wonderful. In fact, I think she thought I was a few eggs short of a dozen since you didn't tell me anything about this job. This house is not creepy. It is beautiful and there is no such thing as a haunted house, and I don't know what you mean by a good kind of haunted. There's a good kind of haunted?"

"Of course," Helen said with a wicked grin. "The kind with ghosts that fall in love with you."

"You are crazy. There are no such things as ghosts."

"You'd be surprised. You shouldn't stay here. You should come with me."

"No. I'm staying. Did you see the library? This place is amazing. I don't believe in hauntings and even if this place is haunted, I can endure a ghost or two to sleep in a such a beautiful room with a view like this."

I started to unpack. I didn't have much and it didn't take me long to find homes for my meager possessions. I tried to ignore Helen watching me from the bed. Her eyebrows were knitted together in concern. It didn't matter to me that the house was a little spooky. All old houses had cobwebs and ghost stories in common. It was part of their charm. Their long histories and dark corners lent themselves to the type of morbid fascination that drew such tall tales. I wouldn't concern myself with fables or folktales. I didn't believe in ghosts or hauntings, and there was nothing that went bump in the night that scared me any more than the things I could see with my own eyes.

When I was done unpacking, I sat on the bed beside Helen. The door opened and a young woman popped her head in and announced dinner. She said she would wait for me in the hall to show me down. I thanked her and turned back to Helen. I couldn't suppress my smile. I was so happy to be there.

Helen shook her head and crossed her arms over her chest. "I'm not going to eat in Creepsville. The food here is probably poisoned."

"Creepsville? If you hate it here so much, why don't you leave?" I matched her stance and crossed my own arms over my chest. "This was your idea. You pushed me to take this job. Why did you bring me here?"

"I didn't know it would be like this. How could I have known? Jane, I can see things you can't. We should leave."

"I can't leave," I whispered. "I have no place to go and even if I did, there is something special about this place."

Helen huffed and stood up. "Girl, you've read waaaaay too many romance novels."

"So what if I have?" I said, flinging my arms wide. "So what if I have big dreams and want something good in my life for a change."

Helen grabbed my hand, her expression desperate. "We've been through a lot in our lives, you and I." She touched my face. "I don't want you to get hurt. I made a mistake with this."

"How can a house hurt me?" I said, shaking my head. "I'm sorry Helen, but this time, you are over-reacting. I need this job. I need a place to live. And I need to get through the next four years so I can finally live my life the way I want to live it."

Helen shook her head. Her lips had thinned in an angry line. "Look, I can't stay here. If you don't want to come with me, then fine. You're on your own then. But I'm outta here."

"Fine!" I said, feeling hurt and mad at the same time.

"Fine!" she replied, and grabbing her bag, she left.

I quickly put the rest of my things away and used the bathroom. Sometimes Helen made me want to scream, she was so stubborn... But I wasn't going to budge. No way. Thornfield was the best thing that had ever happened to me, I could feel it. I blew out a deep breath, left my room, and smiled at the maid who was waiting patiently for me in the hall.

I followed the young woman down the long hall, back downstairs, through the formal dining room, into the huge gourmet kitchen, and finally to a cozy area off the kitchen with a round table set for six people. The scent of thyme and rosemary drifted through the air and my stomach growled in response to the lovely aromas. Food had been a scarce commodity in the Blankenship home. Even though I'd started working from the age of eight as a babysitter, as well as mowing lawns in the summer, before I was old enough to get a job at a local bookstore, most of my earnings had gone to clothes, and school supplies, and books. My food staples consisted of ramen noodles, mac and cheese, and bananas because I needed some nutrients in my diet. I took a stack of plates from a young man and helped set the table.

There were three staff members present. Mrs. Fairfax sat at the head of the table. Jenna was the girl who had announced dinner and she was also the cook. She was older than she looked. She had started talking as she entered the kitchen and seemed unable to stop. She had three children she supported on her own and she cooked and served the meals and then went home. She was tall and heavy set, with a face that could have been almost any age. She had curly dark hair and pretty dark-blue eyes. James was the other staff member. He took care of the horses and helped with minor repairs, as necessary. He looked like he was about twenty-five and he smiled too much for my comfort. He had short blonde hair and big brown eyes that I imagined got him plenty of dates. He was good looking in that boy-next-door kind of way.

Mrs. Fairfax stood up and smiled. "Before dinner is served, I would like to introduce you to Jane Marsh. I hope you will both make her feel at home here. During the day Jane will be attending class at Huntington, but at night she will be Miss Adele's companion. Her duty is to watch over Miss Adele to make sure she is all right."

James stared at me in a way that made me want to crawl under the table and hide. "I would be happy to show you around so you won't get lost… It's easy to get lost in a big place like this with so many dark places…"

"No need," I said bluntly. "Mrs. Fairfax already gave me a tour and I have no problem finding my way around." I returned his creepy leer with a scowl.

Undaunted, he continued staring. "You look something… Are you Mexican or something?"

I hated that question. I wanted to pull my shirt up over my head. "Yes," I lied. "I'm Mexican."

Jenna hit James on the shoulder. They were obviously friends. "That is rude," Jenna commented.

"I had a friend in high school from Mexico City. His name was Garcia. Do you know him?" James continued. He may have been flirting, but I was inexperienced and he was doing it terribly if he was doing it, so I couldn't be sure. I just knew I wanted him to shut up.

"Yes," I said coldly, going into nerd-brain mode, which was how I usually dealt with ignorant people. "Just by being born with dark skin and a Mexican phenotype gives me access to knowing every single person of Mexican heritage in this nation." That shut James up, but it didn't stop him from staring.

Jenna returned to her chit-chat. She talked about Thornfield and babbled on about her personal life. I listened politely and avoided James's eyes.

The door to the kitchen opened and a plump woman in kitten scrubs entered the dining hall guiding an elderly woman who looked like she might have been a century old. Everybody stood up when they entered.

"How are you doing this evening, Miss Adele?" Mrs. Fairfax asked the old woman.

"Fine," Miss Adele smiled. "Beverly has been reading me poetry. That always makes the day better."

Despite my usual reserved nature, I found myself blurting out, "What poems were you reading?"

Miss Adele's gaze turned toward me, but it was clear that she couldn't see me very well. "Who's this?" she asked.

"I'm Jane, Ma'am," I answered. "I'm new here. I'll be staying with you at night."

Miss Adele arched an eyebrow and sat down in her chair. She was so thin a strong wind might snap her in two. Her crepe-paper skin gathered around her skeletal form. Her large, blue eyes peered out into the distance but clearly couldn't make out everything in her environment. She wore a blue track suit and sneakers, and there was a diamond brooch on her lapel. Her hair was a perfect cap of white wavy-curls; the signature style of many an old lady.

Jenna stood up and began serving dinner once Miss Adele was seated. The food was delicious and for a minute, I forgot my manners and dove into the meal like a starving child in a bad depiction of Annie. Suddenly, I remembered myself, sat up straight, and dabbed the napkin at the corners of my mouth, trying not to act like I hadn't just inhaled half a chicken breast.

"So," Miss Adele said in between small bites of chicken, "do you like poetry, Jane?"

"I love poetry," I said. "I love to read."

"That is such a rare gift in these modern youths," Miss Adele said. Her hand shook and she dropped her fork. Beverly, the nurse, picked up Miss Adele's fork and helped her eat.

"There is no place for magic. For magic there is no hope," Miss Adele muttered as she chewed.

I finished her sentence. "Books are its last remembrance. For nowhere else can it cope."

Miss Adele smiled. "It will be nice to have a young person like you in the house. The nights here are so long and dark."

Beverly laughed and spooned another morsel of food into Miss Adele's mouth. "Don't be silly, Miss Adele. You sleep through the night like a log. You're forgetting things again."

Miss Adele was silenced by this and she finished her food quietly. I ate and watched the old woman with curiosity. How could the nurse know if Miss Adele slept through the night if she wasn't with her?

After dinner, Beverly helped Miss Adele back to her room, and there was a bustle of activity as everyone worked together to clear the table. After the kitchen was clean, Jenna scampered off with containers of leftovers. She waved goodbye happily and disappeared. After spending a few extra moments leering at me, James left, too.

Mrs. Fairfax sighed. It was 6:00 p.m.

"We eat dinner early because Miss Adele hates eating alone," Mrs. Fairfax said with a shrug. "Eat with her when you can."

"I'm fine with that," I said.

"The night nurse leaves at eight. The day nurse arrives at five-thirty a.m."

"What should I do if Miss Adele wakes up in the middle of the night?" I asked.

"That won't happen," Mrs. Fairfax answered.

"How do you know that?" I asked. "Shouldn't there be some kind of plan? I mean, you never know what could happen, and I am not a trained nurse."

Mrs. Fairfax placed a bottle of pills in my hand. The bottle was clearly labeled valium.

"Thank you," I said politely.

Mrs. Fairfax smiled. "I hope you believe me when I say it won't be an issue. I understand that you are concerned, but Miss Adele always sleeps through the night. Also, Miss Adele is a sweet woman and will quickly go back to bed if she wakes up. All you have to do is stay in your room at night next door so that Miss Adele knows someone is there."

I nodded. I was happy to let the conversation go. Mrs. Fairfax walked me to the stairs and told me Nurse Beverly would set the security alarm when she finished her shift. Mrs. Fairfax told me she'd finish going through the rest of the household details tomorrow and wished me goodnight. I thanked her and, armed with the bottle of valium, I made my way back upstairs to my bedroom. There was an uncanny quiet about the place once everyone had left. Every small creak was magnified. Every groan in the floorboards sounded like thunder.

Helen was waiting for me in my room. I had no idea when she'd returned, but I was very glad she was back. She sat quietly, cross-legged on the bed, flipping through the pages of a magazine like nothing had happened. "Did the rest of the staff look like The Addam's Family?" she asked.

I shrugged. "They looked more like the family from The Texas Chain Saw Massacre."

Helen nodded. "So, they will probably sacrifice you to something evil in the house and eat you?"

"I'm okay with that," I answered calmly. "But you clearly never saw The Texas Chain Saw Massacre if that is what you think happens in that movie."

Helen laughed. "You know I love you and I only want what's best for you, right?"

I hugged Helen. "Of course I know that!"

She and I settled down on the bed and attempted to make the archaic television work. Sadly, it only got five channels and Helen and I finally resigned ourselves to going to bed early rather than listen to the moaning of the old house.

Helen and I crawled into the enormous bed, pulled the covers up over us, and watched the shadows dance on the ceiling. Sleep seemed impossible. The wind outside the window howled and every noise echoed through the empty halls.

"I'm sorry," Helen said.

"It's okay. I'm sorry we fought, too."

"I shouldn't have gotten you mixed up in this weirdness. I wish I could do this for you."

I looked over at Helen. In the moonlight, she was even prettier. Her skin looked like porcelain and her face had the kind of beauty that romantic poets write about. Helen walked in beauty like the night.

I sighed. "This isn't that weird and why would you be better at this than me?"

"Don't take this the wrong way, but you don't know the real world. You're soft and sweet and that is what I love about you. You're so smart, but you live in your books and weird movies. You wouldn't know what to do if this was some kind of creepy con or hustle."

"I don't know what to say about that really. It's not like you are tough as iron."

Helen's face stiffened in the darkness. "I know how hard the world can be," Helen said in a bitter voice. "There is nothing in this weird house that could hurt me."

"It isn't that weird," I said again.

"The fact that you don't think this house is weird only emphasizes how naïve you are."

"There is no way Mrs. Fairfax could be involved in anything unethical. She's a sweet lady and Miss Adele is delightful."

Helen rolled her eyes. "Really? Adele is delightful?" Sarcasm dripped from Helen's tongue. "Are you even from this planet? Nobody who was born after 1950 talks like that."

"I'm not that naïve," I said.

The shadows above me twisted and turned as the branches of the massive tree outside my window danced in the wind.

"Just be careful and call me if you need anything at all."

I put my hand on my friend's arm and smiled. She was being kind. She liked to watch out for me.

The wind had lulled me into a kind of trance and sleep began to tug at my eyes. Helen curled up next to me with her hand on mine. Her breath was sweet. Slowly, we drifted off to sleep.

CHAPTER 5

All life is only a set of pictures in the brain, among which there is no difference betwixt those born of real things and those born of inward dreamings, and no cause to value the one above the other.

~ H.P. Lovecraft

DREAMS FOLLOWED ME THAT NIGHT. They caught me in their twisted embrace and carried me back to all the things from my childhood that haunted me. I dreamt of the day my second foster mother, Mrs. Reed, kicked me out of her home. I was seven when she threw me out. I had been wild then.

My foster brother, John, had been chasing me all day. I was never sure if he just liked tormenting people or if he had a hatred for me, but torturing me seemed to be his favorite past time. Most of the time he just called me names. Sometimes he would steal my toys or pull my hair. One time, he took my only doll, tore her head off, and used it as a soccer ball in the backyard. That day, I was hiding behind the curtains in the living room. I still remember the book I was reading. A Wrinkle in Time. I think I was born being able to read. From the age of five, I was reading the kinds of books that most people read in high school or university. I was so lost in the book that I forgot to listen for John. I forgot that I should be afraid. He pulled back the curtains and snatched my book.

"Where'd you get this?" he taunted. "Did you steal it?"

"I got it from the library," I said with my chin held high in defiance. "If you knew how to read, you'd know about libraries." I knew I was going to regret it the moment I'd said it.

"What did you say, you terrible little mooch?" John's face was red with rage.

"I said, if you knew how to read, you'd know about libraries."

John hit me. He hit me so hard I went spinning to the floor. I saw stars and my head buzzed. While I lay on the ground, he kicked me in the stomach. All I could hear was his laughter. He laughed and he tore the pages from my book. I don't remember deciding to act. I just remember anger. Anger washed over me like a tsunami. I lunged at him and knocked him off his feet. He fell backward and I pounded him with my fists. He began to scream and cry.

Mrs. Reed came in and pulled me off her son. Her face twisted in rage. Her hot pink lips pursed together in disgust. John was her real son, but she'd taken in three foster kids, me and two other girls. The other girls were six and eight and had straight blonde hair and blue eyes. My hair was "wild" according to Mrs. Reed. She had such a hard time with it she took me to the hairdresser one day and told them to chop it all off. She said it was "too kinky" and matted. But Lydia and Kitty had baby-fine hair that Mrs. Reed could easily braid or put into barrettes. The two girls could have been blood sisters, they looked so much alike. They spent most of their time having pretend tea parties and playing with their dolls. They never misbehaved. "Why don't you act more like Lydia and Kitty?" Mrs. Reed would scold me. "They know how to get adopted." That's what Mrs. Reed always told me.

But on that day, Mrs. Reed was beyond scolding. She was so mad her face had turned purple. I had harmed her precious son.

"You are a despicable little girl," she hissed. "I should have never taken you in. You are nothing but a freak. What kind of child has tattoos? I bet your parents were Satanists and the Devil lives inside you. You are a nothing but a little porch monkey with parents who probably practiced Voodoo. I should have never taken in a black girl. "

She grabbed me by my ear and dragged me to the back room. It was a dusty place that her real son said was haunted by the ghost of a woman who had killed herself. I had never believed them, but when I heard Mrs. Reed lock the door, every story he'd told me swirled through my mind. My fevered, childish imagination overflowed with those horrible images. I could hear laughing in the darkness. It was wicked laughter. It was laughter filled with evil and I banged my fists against the splintered wood of the door. I screamed out and begged for help, but the door remained locked. It wasn't a ghost that came for me in that room. It was a man with horns. His skin was dark and his eyes glowed yellow in the darkness. The devil came and as his cackle filled the room, I sat on the floor with my hands over my ears rocking back and forth...

I woke up drenched in sweat in my beautiful and elegant bedroom at Thornfield. My nightgown clung to my body. Oddly, the evil laughter still echoed around me. I looked around. It was after midnight. The room was dark except for the moonlight peeking in through the window curtains. Helen was still sound asleep next to me, which was odd considering the wicked laughter was so loud. I got up and opened the window, heavy, Southern June air filled the room. I listened for a moment and confirmed that the cackling was, in fact, coming from somewhere inside the house. Panicked, I immediately thought of Adele and opened my bedroom door.

Miss Adele was standing in the hall. She seemed to be in some kind of trance, but she wasn't the one laughing. I flicked on the hall light and reached for her hand.

"What is it?" I asked her. "What's wrong Miss Adele?"

"It's a dream," she whispered in a trance-like voice. "It's always the same dream."

I gently guided Adele back to her room and helped her into her bed. I was immensely grateful for the valium Mrs. Fairfax had given me. I ran back to my room and grabbed the bottle and a glass of water from the sink. I gave Adele the valium and tucked her into her bed.

Adele's trance-like state seemed to fade and sanity flowed back into her eyes. "It is a dream?" she asked. "Isn't it?"

"Of course." I pulled the covers up over her. I wondered if the night caretakers in the past had slept so soundly they never knew if Miss Adele woke up at night or if they'd lied to cover up what was going on. I had no real idea, but it made me mad to think that Miss Adele might have been wandering around the house alone in a trance for years and no one had bothered to take care of her.

As Adele drifted off to sleep, I noticed the laughter had faded away. I looked out into the hall. All the lights were off and there was only darkness. Not a sound to be heard. I went back into Miss Adele's room. It was smaller than mine but just as nice. The soft nightlight glowed from a plug by the floor bathing the room in a gentle, yellow light. A pretty floral wallpaper adorned the walls and a chintz-covered chaise lounge and two upholstered chairs sat in front of a cozy fireplace. A rocking chair covered with a heavy quilt faced the window overlooking the garden and pool. Several books sat on a small table beside the rocker. The only items that indicated Miss Adele was in poor health were the large hospital bed and the medicine bottles spread out on the antique dresser. I made sure the covers were tucked under her chin and closed the door behind me. I walked back to my own room. The laughter was gone, but I felt distinctly unsettled.

As I crawled into bed, I resolved never to tell Helen about what had happened. She would flip out if she knew that the house was haunted by weird laughs and wandering old ladies. Helen was entirely too sensitive. It took me a while to fall asleep, but when I did, I dreamt of being locked in that old room again, with nothing but wicked laughter and the devil to keep me company.

CHAPTER 6

*The process of delving into the black abyss is
to me the keenest form of fascination.*

~ H.P. Lovecraft

AFTER THAT FIRST STRANGE NIGHT at Thornfield,
my life thankfully fell into a comfortable routine. Helen left
the next day to move into her boyfriend's place, and I got
to know my way around Thornfield and the nearby campus
before school started. I didn't see Helen much after that.
She tended to disappear from time to time and I didn't
question it. I loved her and was grateful for the time she
gave me. Without my friend, I was free to lose myself in
the beauty of my new home.

I spent my mornings exploring Thornfield's enormous
library and enjoyed wandering around the gardens and
strolling through the hedge maze in the late summer sun.
I felt like the heroine from a classic novel. In truth, my
first few weeks at Thornfield were the most relaxing I had
ever had in my life. I didn't have chores to do other than
make sure Adele was okay and slept through the nights. No

more mishaps since that first night. I didn't have any school work to do, yet. I had several weeks until school started. I couldn't remember the last time I hadn't juggled a couple of part-time jobs and my studies and my housework. Some afternoons, I would be bold and slip on the bikini Helen had convinced me to buy. Making certain that the creepy James wasn't around, I would stretch out in the sun by the pool and pretend I was a girl like Helen. I pretended I was beautiful and that the boys were mesmerized by me. I imagined I was an heiress lounging at a resort with nothing better to do than watch the waves crash on the shore. I wasn't afraid of people judging me for my tattoo because there was no one to see it. I could bare everything and I had nothing to fear. I even got a tan. My skin darkened and made it harder for me to see my tattoo. I was happy about that. I had no reason to leave Thornfield. It was perfect.

I kept to myself during those days. I ate my meals with Miss Adele and the other staff. I smiled and laughed at their jokes, but I tried not to linger in conversation. Thornfield was so huge, nobody knew where I was or what I was doing. The staff was small and kept to themselves. Once a week, a big cleaning crew came in and spent the entire day removing dust and keeping the house immaculate, and a landscaping crew swept over the massive grounds making sure there wasn't a twig out of place. I made sure I was out on those days, either exploring Huntington campus or the town. It was easy for me just to do my thing and go the entire day without seeing the rest of the tiny staff. But one afternoon, Miss Adele found me in the library. I had been at Thornfield a little over three weeks and she came in with her cane and sat down beside me in the light of a wide stained-glass window. The sun passing through the glass created a tapestry of dancing color on the hardwood floor.

"Be a dear and get me a copy of Wuthering Heights?" She was out of breath, no doubt from walking through the enormous house. It had taken me a while to become familiar with the entire collection in the library, but I found my way around after the first week. I climbed up the winding staircase and used a narrow ladder to find a lovely elegant leather-bound edition of Wuthering Heights. I handed the book to her and she clutched it in her thin, wrinkled hands.

"Have you read it?" she asked me.

"Many times," I responded.

"I read it many times in my youth," Miss Adele said quietly. "But, at my age, the memory fades. I realized I couldn't even remember the heroine's name anymore. Can you imagine that?"

"Her name is Cathy."

"Of course, of course. What was your name again, dear?"

"I'm Jane."

"You are a pleasant girl, but don't you have friends to be with? It seems like young people always have friends. The other girls always had friends they spent their days with."

"I have a friend, Helen, remember from my first night here? She moved in with her boyfriend and started a part-time job. I start school in a little over a month. I thought I would just relax and read until school starts. Is that okay with you?"

"Yes, dear." Miss Adele patted my arm. "I like you. I like you much more than the other girls. You don't play loud music or wear short skirts. You like books. I like you."

I smiled. "I like you, too."

Miss Adele smiled. She closed her eyes for a minute and I thought she had drifted off to sleep, but then she opened them again. "In my youth, I spent all my days in this room. Of course, that was before computers and color televisions with a thousand channels, and all these other electronic doohickies you young people spend your time with now. In my day, a room like this was all a girl needed."

"I guess I should have lived in your day because this is all I need, too."

Miss Adele's nurse came bursting through the door with a panicked look on her face. She heaved a huge sigh of relief when she saw Adele sitting beside me. It wasn't Beverly or one of the other nurses I had met before. No wonder Miss Adele was so confused all the time. I would be, too. She seemed to have a different nurse every day.

"Don't you run off on me like that," the nurse chastised. "I've been looking all over for you, Miss Adele. You could have got hurt."

"Nonsense," Miss Adele responded. "I'm a grown woman and this is my house. If I want to come sit in my own library, then I will do so."

"Now Miss Adele, you know you need me to come with you. Come on now. It's time for your nap."

The nurse helped the elderly woman to her feet and dragged her out of the library, leaving me alone once again.

A breeze passed by me. I was surprised by the sudden chill. I looked around, but the windows were closed. Another whoosh of wind passed me and, with it, the eerie sound of distant laughter.

CHAPTER 7

*Ocean is more ancient than the mountains,
and freighted with the memories and the
dreams of Time.*

~ H. P. Lovecraft

I STARTED SCHOOL IN EARLY September. The days passed much more quickly once I had classes to contend with. I took a full course load and buried myself in my studies. I could have lost myself in school and never come up for air if it weren't for the necessity of extracurricular activities to round out my inevitable and eventual application to med school. With this in mind, I joined the Biology Club. The first meeting was torture as the group admins went through all the rules and what was expected of everyone. The second meeting was a party. That was worse than torture.

I entered the party quietly and tried to blend in with the wallpaper. The Biology Club meeting room had been transformed into a summer garden and every corner was full of plants, branches, and vines that the committee had gathered from the forested grounds behind the college. I found a leafy corner to sit in. I wished I'd brought a book. I looked around at everyone chatting and mingling. I saw one couple kissing in a corner. I wondered what it felt like to be kissed. I'd never been kissed except once by a boy in my high school. The boy had been kind and I had been terrible. I tutored him in chemistry. I was so young. I started high school when I was twelve and it rarely registered with anyone how young I was. I was a sophomore and barely fourteen when the boy had swept me into his arms and kissed me. He was eighteen and a senior. I had gasped and run off. I stopped tutoring him after that. I suppose I'd hurt his feelings, but I didn't know how to react. He told me I was beautiful. I thought he was a liar.

About an hour after I'd arrived at the party, a slender boy with brown hair and glasses came and sat down beside me.

"Hey," he said awkwardly.

"Hey," I answered with equal awkwardness.

"I haven't seen you here before," he said.

"I'm a freshman."

"Oh. I'm guessing you're a biology major?"

"Premed."

"Are you staying on campus?"

"I'm staying at Thornfield Hall," I answered without thinking. It occurred to me that I shouldn't tell strangers where I lived. Although, I wasn't sure why.

"Really?" he asked with sudden enthusiasm. "The haunted house?"

"It's not haunted. And besides, I don't believe in ghosts."

"Didn't that guy murder his girlfriend up there? What's his name? Edward Rochester. Didn't he cut her up and set her on fire?"

Inwardly, I was shocked that such a terrible rumor had been circulating. Who would say such awful things about the Rochester family and why? The only Rochester I had met was Miss Adele and she was just a sweet old lady.

"That's absolutely absurd," I said with bravado.

"They say that all the Rochester men end up murdering their wives, but Edward, the youngest Rochester started early and killed his girlfriend. That's why he doesn't go to Huntington. They sent him away to Yale."

I'm sure my face registered my shock and disapproval because the boy with the glasses suddenly went mute and became even more awkward. I didn't care about ghost stories or urban legends, and I wasn't good at pretending I did.

"Sorry," I said stiffly. "I don't know anything about that."

"Where are you from?" he asked, trying to shift the conversation.

"Massachusetts," I answered. I knew where he was going with his line of questioning before the next question came. I wanted to dig a hole and crawl into it.

"Yeah, but where are your parents from?" he pushed.

"Massachusetts."

"Where are your people from?" he continued.

Why did everyone need to put me in an ethnic box? Why couldn't I just be me, Jane Marsh, and leave it at that? "Michigan," I lied.

He nodded and shifted uncomfortably. I would have given anything to escape. It occurred to me that Thornfield was only a short walking distance away. I only needed the Biology Club to round out my application. No one would ever know if I left every event early.

"I want to go into ornithology," he said.

I had no idea how I should respond to that, so I just nodded and smiled. The uncomfortable conversation continued for a few minutes and then the boy drifted back into the sea of people. I took his departure as my cue to leave. I ran out into the night and left the party behind me. I felt like I was escaping prison. The fresh air was made even sweeter in comparison to the stifling air inside the crowded party.

It was a beautiful night and the neo-gothic buildings made me feel like I was walking through a European city. The stars were bright and the moon glowed as I made my way back to Thornfield. As I walked past the biology building I saw the old cemetery tucked away behind it. I'd seen it every day on my way to and from class, but never had the time to stop. It wasn't much and it sat between the biology department and a wooded area that shrouded Thornfield Hall. It was an easy path to take on my way home. I walked through the cemetery. I always liked graveyards. They were quiet. The stones told stories. This was the old Rochester family cemetery. Every name on every stone ended in Rochester. A stone angel, worn thin by time, stood watch over the tiny necropolis. I wondered why no one tended the cemetery. Why it had been abandoned. I understood that feeling. I had lived with it my entire life.

I glanced at my watch. Mrs. Fairfax had told me I could have Friday evenings to myself as long as I made it home by midnight. But after my first experience at the Biology Club party, I probably wouldn't take her up on that offer again. I turned and continued on my way, leaving the cemetery to the moon and the stars.

The gate to Thornfield was always locked after the staff left. I took out my keys and unlocked it, letting myself back onto the property. The walk down the driveway was the longest part of my walk. There were no lamps to guide my way, and the dense cover of the trees that lined the drive made it hard to see.

I was wearing my best dress. It was white and long with long sleeves. It covered my tattoo well and I think that's why I liked it. It billowed around me in the darkness exposing my skin to the cool, night air. I quickened my pace in an attempt to make it home faster. The wind rustled through the trees. In the distance, another noise became apparent. It was a pounding noise like a horse's hooves. The hairs on the back of my neck stood up. I walked faster and then I was running. The thundering sound grew louder and louder. I sprinted to the side of the path and glanced over my shoulder. All I could see were two crazed black eyes of an animal. And then someone yelled. I screamed and tripped over the root of a tree. I shut my eyes and lay in the dirt trying to catch my breath.

CH⅄PTER 8

I have seen the dark universe yawning.
Where the black planets roll without aim,
where they roll in their horror unheeded,
without knowledge, or luster, or name.

~ H.P. Lovecraft

WHEN I OPENED MY EYES, I saw a black horse standing above a man lying in the dirt to my left. I stood up and dusted myself off. I felt stupid. Someone riding a horse had just scared the snot out of me. Granted, whoever it was could be a murderer, but what kind of murderer rode a horse? I walked over to the man. His leg looked injured and he was struggling to stand up. He groaned in pain and fell back down. I didn't recognize him as a staff member at Thornfield.

"You shouldn't be here," I said as I stood over him.

In the dark, his features were hard to see. He seemed young. He had dark hair and he was tall.

"You're crazy!" he bellowed. "It's you who shouldn't be here!"

"I work here. What're you doing here?"

He seemed to calm down after that. He dusted himself off and looked at me.

"I thought you were a ghost. You spooked my horse. But you don't look like a ghost up close. At least not what a ghost is supposed to look like." There was a twinkle in his eyes that suggested he had gone from angry to joking. He was a strange young man. He rode alone at night and could go from furious to ridiculous in three seconds.

I laughed despite myself. "I don't think I am a ghost. I live here."

I could feel him studying me in the dark. "Are you the new night companion for Adele?"

"Who wants to know?" I asked him. "For all I know you're a thief or a murderer. In fact, I should probably call the police or—"

"I'm Edward," he interrupted. "Edward Rochester."

"Oh!" I felt even more stupid than I had felt running from noises in the dark. I had never behaved so foolishly. I had just insulted my boss. I rushed to his side and tried to help him. "I had no idea," I said as I helped him to his feet.

Edward put his arm around my shoulders and leaned on me as I helped him up. He was tall and lanky with broad shoulders. He was built like a swimmer and must have been over 6'4". I felt like a dwarf next to him, even though I was 5'9".

"Can you help me with my horse?" He looked at me and his eyes reflected the moonlight. "Can you help me get her to the stable?"

I nodded and helped him walk over to his horse. He patted her flank and whispered softly to her. Anyone who was nice to animals must be a good person. I knew that as sure as I knew there was a tattoo of a door on my back.

I helped Edward back to the stable and we left the horse in a small enclosed area. It was clear he lacked the strength to put her in a stall. I thought they were called stalls. I didn't really know what you did with a horse, but he seemed upset that he was just leaving her outside.

"She'll be safe enough here tonight," Edward said as he undid her saddle. He grimaced in pain and I helped him lift it off and lay it on the ground of the shed. "I'll have to send James out for her first thing in the morning." He gave me another intense look that could only be described as a ferocious frown. He started making his way out of the shed and almost toppled to the ground. "What're you doing out at this time of night anyway?" he growled. "Making a guy fall off his horse? Shouldn't you be in with my grandmother?"

"I'm sorry," I said as I helped him back onto the driveway that led to the house. "Mrs. Fairfax said I could have the evening off to go to a party if I was back by midnight. She's in with Miss Adele now."

"That's no excuse for you wandering around at night. Don't you have any sense?"

"I like to walk," I said.

"In the middle of the night by yourself? In the woods? It's not safe."

"I enjoy the fresh air."

We finally made it to the house and I helped Edward to the study. I ran up the stairs and through the house to the sitting room across from Miss Adele's room. Mrs. Fairfax sat in the room sipping a glass of wine and watching an old game show I didn't recognize. She smiled but her smile faded when she saw the state of me.

"My goodness! What happened to you? Are you all right?"

"Edward's back!" I exclaimed. "I almost killed him and now he has a broken leg."

"Oh dear," Mrs. Fairfax said. "I'll call the doctor. He'll come out for Edward. He's an old family friend. You should go keep Edward company. He gets in quite a state sometimes and you can help calm him down."

"I don't think he'll want to talk to me."

Mrs. Fairfax took her cell phone out of her pocket. "Why not?"

I shrugged. "He doesn't like me."

"Never mind that. He doesn't like anyone. He's usually in a bad mood. He comes and goes as he pleases and works everyone up into a frenzy when he's here. Ignore his manners. He's never had any."

I stood in the doorway for a moment just staring at Mrs. Fairfax. I wanted to go see Edward even less than ever. I felt awful for causing his accident. I really wanted to keep my job and I was scared that if I went downstairs he would fire me. I hoped that if I stood in the doorway long enough, maybe Mrs. Fairfax would tell me to sit down and that she'd go talk to Edward. My plan didn't work.

"Run along. I've got a thousand calls to make. Edward expects a full staff and I have to make sure they are all here by 5 a.m. Go, go, before he gets even madder and then there'll be hell to pay," Mrs. Fairfax commanded.

Mrs. Fairfax looked anxious. I had never seen her look anything but pleasant. The fact that she looked so nervous made me feel even worse. I walked as slowly as I could. I dragged my feet all the way back to the study, but I couldn't put it off forever. I would eventually have to face the young man I had managed to disable in the first five minutes of meeting. I would have to face my boss. I peeked around the corner and tried to avoid being seen. I could see Edward in the lamplight, lying on a leather couch and reading a book. For a moment, I was taken aback. I couldn't see him very well when we'd been outside, and I avoided looking at him when we'd come into the house. He was strikingly hand-some. I knew he was at Yale, so he couldn't have been older than about twenty or twenty-one, but he seemed so much more mature. He had a strong jaw and high cheekbones. His hair was thick and black, and his eyes looked light-colored, but I couldn't quite tell from where I was standing. He was slightly disheveled, and his clothes, although dirt-stained, were fancy: riding pants and jacket and shiny black boots.

"Are you going to stand in the doorway all night or are you going to come in?" he asked, his eyes still on the pages of his book. My cheeks turned bright red in embarrassment at being caught staring.

"I'm s-sorry," I stuttered. "Mrs. Fairfax has called for the doctor."

"You should be," he said. "You made me fall off my horse and ruined a good night. Are you sure you aren't a ghost here to haunt me?"

I shook my head.

"Sit down. You make me nervous standing over me like that."

I sat immediately. I collapsed into a chair across from him. Edward looked up and pinned me with his gaze. His eyes were blue like Helen's, but where hers were a solid blue, his had flecks of green. They were startling to look at. I had never seen such eyes before. He stared at me the way someone would stare at a painting or sculpture. He scowled and I blushed in response to his scrutiny. People rarely looked at me. Except when they were trying to figure out my heritage. I suppose I probably looked awful. My only decent dress was torn and covered in muck. My face felt stiff from dirt caked on it and my hair was tangled with weeds.

I liked being ignored. It was what I was used to. Having him stare at me made me wish I could disappear. Fade away into the wallpaper. But at least he didn't stare like James did. Aside from dinner, I tried to avoid James at every turn. I only hung out by the pool when I knew he was working on the other side of the property. When I was around James, he would leer at me like he could see me naked. I had no idea why he was so interested in me. I guess it was because I was the only young, single girl in the house most days.

Edward's stare wasn't leering. It was analytical, like he was trying to figure me out.

"What depressing story brings you to Thornfield?" he asked after a while.

"What?" I asked in confusion. "I don't have a sad story." Well, I actually did have a sad story, but I didn't like to talk about myself either, and I certainly wasn't going to spill my guts to a virtual stranger, even if he was my boss.

"All the other girls had sad stories. They were all desperate for money. They were desperate enough to work here. They were miserable."

"I'm not desperate. I like Thornfield and I like Miss Adele. It's beautiful here."

"I've never heard that before."

"Why? Thornfield is breathtaking. I could spend a lifetime in the library alone."

Edward's scowl faded and he actually smiled. He had a beautiful smile. It was wide and warm, and it made me feel like I was floating. I smiled back at him. I couldn't help myself. At that moment, I completely understood what all sixteen-year-old girls feel when they meet a cute guy with a great smile and gorgeous blue eyes.

"No one ever notices how beautiful it is here anymore," Edward said. "They only believe those stupid stories. I always thought it was beautiful, too."

"I don't know why anyone would waste their time with ghost stories and urban legends. It's their loss."

Edward's smile faded a bit and he stared at me again. "You're different from all the other girls," he said more to himself than to me.

"Does your leg hurt much?" I asked, trying to keep up the polite conversation, even though I could feel my stomach doing flip-flops. How was I different from all the other girls? Were they nicer? Smarter? Prettier? I suddenly wished I looked like Helen and not like myself. Everything about Helen was vibrant. Everything about me was not.

"Not much," he answered. "So, if you don't have a sad story that brought you here, where are you from? Why are you working here?

"I have a scholarship to Huntington, but it doesn't cover room and board. I had saved up the money I needed, but my foster mother was going to lose her house, so I gave all the money I had to her so she could keep it. My friend found this job for me and since it includes room and board, it will help me save for med school. It's perfect."

What just happened? I opened my mouth and my entire life story poured out and I couldn't stop. Somewhere in between his eyes and my flip flopping stomach I told this stranger more about myself than I had told anyone except Helen.

"Your foster mother? Where's your real mother and father? Couldn't they have helped you?"

"I don't know where they are. I never knew them."

"And you say you don't have a sad story?"

"There are a lot of people with much sadder stories."

"Yeah, but your story is still sad."

Mrs. Fairfax came in with a glass of water and a bottle of aspirin. "The doctor will be here any minute now," she said as she gave Edward the glass of water and the pills.

She turned and looked at me. "It's late, run along to bed." And in a whisper added, "Don't tell Miss Adele about this mishap, we don't want to worry her."

I nodded like a bobble-head doll and sprinted out of the room I had never been more relieved to escape a conversation in my life. I felt like I was a medical specimen and Edward was dissecting me. I wasn't comfortable talking about myself. Helen was the only person in my life who knew anything in depth about me.

I reached my bedroom, out of breath and my heart was pounding. I put my hand on my face. I was flushed. I wanted to cry and I couldn't explain why. It was just a conversation. People had conversations every day. People talked about their lives. It was normal. But I wasn't normal. My parents had been drug addicts and freaks. That's what Mrs. Reed had told me over and over again. I had been shipped from foster home to foster home until Mrs. Blankenship's, and while she had never lifted a hand in anger toward me, she hadn't really talked to me, either. Never asked me how I was doing in school or how my day went. I had lived in the same house with her for six years of my life, but we were virtual strangers.

I looked in the bathroom mirror. My eye makeup had smeared. I looked like a train wreck. I washed my face and took off my soiled dress. I took a shower and scrubbed myself until I felt normal again. I put my yoga pants on and pulled a gray t-shirt over my head. I climbed into bed and tried to erase the conversation from my thoughts. But Edward's eyes... I couldn't get them out of my head. I couldn't get his smile out of my head or the way he looked at me when I talked. I pulled the covers over me, embarrassed by my reaction to him. Eventually, I was able to calm down and fall asleep.

My sleep was fitful. I dreamt of a dark place with old trees. It was quiet and filled with little creatures I could not quite identify. I walked along a winding path for what seemed like hours. Finally, I came upon an old house with a red door. I felt a hand on my shoulder. I turned and saw him. The only man I had ever dreamed of. He was tall and handsome, with black hair and dark skin. His skin looked like wood; mahogany, perhaps. He looked like he was part of a tree, as if he was something born of the woods. He was beautiful. He smiled at me. A charming, Hollywood A-list actor kind of smile. He had ram's horns growing out of his head. And I knew he was evil. I opened my mouth to scream, but no sound came out.

CHAPTER 9

*No new horror can be more terrible than the
daily torture of the commonplace.*

~ H.P. Lovecraft

"DON'T BE AFRAID," HE SAID.

I tried to run, but I couldn't move. I looked down and saw why. Roots had grown out of my arms and legs, anchoring me to the dark soil. I looked back up at the devil man.

"Soon." He smiled again. "I will see you soon. Don't be afraid. It will be beautiful."

I woke up clawing at my legs. I couldn't move. I looked down and saw the blankets had twisted around me. I sighed in relief. Just a bad dream. A stupid bad dream.

Then I heard it. The laughing. For a second I thought I was still dreaming, but then I realized it was coming from somewhere in the house. I opened my bedroom door half expecting to see Miss Adele wandering the halls again, but the hallway was empty. I looked in on her and was relieved that she was sound asleep. Closing her door quietly behind me, I followed the sound of the laughter down the long hall into a part of the mansion I hadn't yet explored. I followed it to a door that was ajar. I peeked behind the door with both fear and curiosity. I thought it was a door to a room, but what I discovered was a set of stairs that climbed up into darkness.

I turned on the light switch at the bottom of the stairs and made my way up. The laughter grew louder. A sudden breeze took me by surprise and I shivered. I could see my breath in front of me. It formed an icy cloud. The drop in temperature seemed odd considering the weather was still warm, even at night, but I kept going. Fear pulsed through my limbs, but I wouldn't be deterred. I needed to find out what the source of this laughter was. I had heard it one too many times. What could produce such diabolical cackle? Was it a person or was there really a ghost at Thornfield?

I reached the top of the stairs and found myself in some kind of tower bedroom. The walls were rounded and there was one window in the room with heavy curtains. A large mahogany bed sat at one end. It had curtains covered with depictions of dragons on it. There was also a fireplace and a dresser. The fireplace was black with soot and covered in cobwebs. The light above me flickered and faded; the room got darker and my teeth began to chatter with cold. There were no doors, other than the door from where I had come.

The laughter started again. There was no other place the sound could be coming from. It was so loud I put my hands over my ears. It was everywhere. Ghost stories filled my mind. I remembered watching a scary old movie called The Innocents late one night when I was living with Mrs.

Blankenship. And now, the haunting tale of that movie floated through my mind. And what about the rumors of Thornfield being haunted? Was it true? The laughter grew louder and I removed my hands from my ears.

"What do you want?" I yelled.

The laughter suddenly stopped. The light flickered again and grew very bright, and the room flooded with the stuffy warmth you would expect from an attic. I opened the curtains and looked out the window. The university campus and the mountains beyond were worthy of a picture. I imagined that this tower room must have been the most beautiful room at Thornfield in its day. I scolded myself for succumbing to my fears.

My curiosity came back full force, and I opened the dresser and found several notebooks filled with sketches. They were all beautiful. I smiled despite myself and blushed. They were sketches of Edward. He was so handsome, just looking at the pictures of him made my cheeks turn red.

A scream filled the night air and I dropped the notebook. It wasn't a woman and it wasn't like the laughter. It was a man yelling. I ran down the stairs as quickly as I could and stumbled into the hall. The yelling stopped, but the hall was filled with so much smoke I had to put my hand over my mouth to breathe. I followed the smoke to a room and ran in. The bed curtains in Edward's room were on fire and he was sound asleep in the middle of his bed. I wondered how anyone could sleep through such chaos and then I saw the empty beer bottles on his nightstand and understood.

I ran to Edward and shook him. He was sleeping like the dead. I pulled the blankets off of him and began to drag him off the bed. He seemed even heavier than when I had helped him back to the house. He felt like a boulder. I was worried I would reinjure his leg, but I kept pulling. It didn't matter. I had to move him. He hit the floor with a loud thud and he finally woke up. His striking blue eyes opened and he looked up at me and then he looked at the fire around him. He stood up and grabbed me. He literally lifted me off my feet and carried me from the room. He carried me down the hall and set me down once we were passed the smoke. I coughed and fell to the ground. The smoke was so thick I could hardly breathe. Edward ran down the hall and came back with a fire extinguisher. I closed my eyes. My eyes were burning. My lungs were burning. All I could do was cough and lie on the floor.

I became aware that I was in Edward's arms again. He was carrying me down the hall like a princess in an old fairy tale. I put my arms around him and leaned into him. I didn't dare open my eyes. I coughed again and felt gently placed on the sofa in the sitting room. He didn't let me go. He still held me.

"Are you okay?" he asked.

I nodded.

"Open your eyes and let me look at you," he commanded.

I opened my eyes and squirmed off of his lap. My heart was racing. I pushed myself as far away from him as I could get and looked at him. He was shirtless and wearing a pair of boxers. His body was perfect, and just looking at him made me blush again. I looked away from him, but I could feel him studying me.

"Thank you," he said. "I think I might have had too much to drink. I would have died if you hadn't come in. You saved my life."

"I heard you yelling," I said softly. I was afraid of my own voice.

He shook his head. "I never yelled."

"There was laughter and then I heard you yelling." My eyes were still burning and the room was spinning. I felt light-headed. I must have breathed in more smoke than I remembered. I wondered how I had been able to make it all the way down the hall and pull Edward from his bed. I was hardly able to stand. Edward's face was blurry.

I could see Edward frown through the haze of my watering eyes. He seemed upset. "You must have been dreaming."

I shook my head. "I was awake. I heard yelling."

"You are very brave," he said, almost gently.

I looked over at him and gasped when I noticed his arm. It was covered in angry blisters. Black soot painted his torso a dingy gray. His hair was disheveled. The smell of burnt skin lingered in the room.

I tried to stand up. I had to get bandages for his arm. I knew where the nurse kept her supplies. I had to get ice. I had read that burns needed ice. I stood up and my head felt dizzy. I tried to take a step forward, but it was like walking through a fog. And then everything went black.

CHAPTER 10

*I felt myself on the edge of the world;
peering over the rim into a fathomless
chaos of eternal night.*

~ H.P. Lovecraft

I WOKE UP IN MY bed. The smell of smoke was gone and I was wearing a clean nightgown. My eyes weren't burning and the sun shone brightly. Had the fire been a dream? And Edward? Had he been a dream, too? I showered, dressed, and left my room. I wasn't sure what to expect.

As I walked down the hall, I saw that the night had been real. Servants I didn't recognize were in the hall pulling out the burnt remains of Edward's bed curtains. The room was filled with maids scrubbing the black soot from the walls and contractors repairing the fire damage from the night before. I kept my head down and tried to make it to the kitchen without being noticed. This proved to be an impossible feat. The house was filled with people. I had no idea who they were, but they all seemed to be bustling about. My quiet sanctuary had become Grand Central Station.

I managed to make it to the staff kitchen without talking to anyone and was just about to sit down for breakfast when Mrs. Fairfax grabbed me by the arm.

"My dear, are you all right?" She looked anxious. Her brow was knit with worry.

"Yes, I'm fine, thank you." I smiled, trying to reassure her.

"You are a very brave girl!" She squeezed my hand. "Edward phoned me about the fire. It must have started in the fireplace in his room. He was reading by the fire and when he went to bed, the book must have fallen off the table. These old houses and their old fireplaces you know. We must be very careful not to leave anything flammable near those open flames.

I nodded in agreement. I hadn't thought about how the fire had started. It didn't make any sense to me, but what did I know? "What's going on?" I asked. "Why are all these people here?"

"Edward invited some friends from Yale to stay with him next week. He wants the house in order. It is ridiculous, of course. Most of the rooms in this house haven't been used since Edward's parents died. I had to hire an entire team of temps to complete the work. I think he's lost his mind. I don't know what he could be thinking. We don't see him for months and then he appears out of nowhere and says he's bringing twenty friends for a party. It's insanity."

"Is there anything I can do to help?"

"No dear," Mrs. Fairfax sighed. "I would say you could take the next two weeks off, but Edward wants you to stay.

I have no idea why. Miss Adele certainly won't be alone and in need of a night companion, but Edward was quite insistent.

"I'll do my best to stay out of everyone's way."

"That would be for the best. Lord only knows what these friends of his are going to be like. He's such a strange young man. They might all have green spiky hair and piercings."

"I'll get my breakfast and eat it in my room."

"I'm sorry, darling. He wants you to eat with him and Miss Adele in the dining room."

I took a deep breath. "Why on Earth would he want me to eat with him?"

"I have no idea. That boy is a mystery."

"The big dining room?" I asked with a sigh. I had walked through the big dining room. I had no desire to eat there. The table in that room was longer than the length of Mrs. Blankenship's house. One piece of china off that table was probably worth more than a year's tuition. I was not the type of girl who should be eating in that dining room.

Mrs. Fairfax must have noticed my discomfort. She put a reassuring hand on my shoulder. "Don't worry. He's strange, but he won't bite," she said with a small smile.

I nodded and turned to go. I had no idea why Edward would want to eat with me. I was nothing but a servant, and not a very important servant at that. I was an ordinary girl without anything interesting to say to a guy in his world. I wished Helen were with me. She would dazzle him with her clever conversation. She would flash her stunning smile, he would be bewitched, and I could fade into the wallpaper.

I made it to the dining room and opened the door. Edward was sitting at one end of the long table and Miss Adele was sitting at the other end. Her nurse was standing behind her and Edward was helping her eat. I felt like I had tripped and fallen into an episode of Downton Abbey. I shuffled my feet uncomfortably in the doorway. I wasn't entirely sure which way to go. I didn't think people lived like this anymore.

"Sit down," Edward commanded. He looked angry. He always looked a little angry. It was easy to see why people didn't like him. Even though I had seen a glimpse of something tender in him last night.

I sat down next to Miss Adele, as far away from Edward as I could.

Edward took a sip of coffee and stared at me with his intense blue eyes. "My grandmother was just telling me about you. She says you're the brightest girl she's ever met."

"Th-thank you." I smiled at Adele.

"She says you're studying medicine."

"No," I corrected. "I'm not studying medicine." He had clearly forgotten that I already mentioned to him that I was saving up for med school. But why would he remember anything I'd told him anyway? I was inconsequential in his life. "I'm just a freshman. I'm taking my core classes now and I'm only pre-med. I'm really not that interesting."

Miss Adele smiled at me. "Oh, don't be silly," she said. "You are the most interesting girl we've had here. You skipped two grades and you are the smartest young person I know. I told him about your love for books and how you saved me from the ghost that haunts my room at night."

"Enough of that," Miss Adele's nurse scolded. Another nurse I didn't recognize. "You know there are no ghosts."

"Well, it seems that Jane likes to wander the halls at night saving people," Edward commented.

I blushed again. I had been blushing so much I thought my face might turn permanently red. Edward must've thought I came from a long line of cherry tomatoes. "I just got lucky last night," I said.

"Luck would have taken you to my room, but it wouldn't have given you the courage to walk through fire and pull me from my bed."

One of the new servants put a plate of eggs and bacon in front of me. I smiled at the girl and said, "Thank you." I didn't feel much like eating. My head hurt a little and I just wanted to go back to my room. Edward was shoveling forkfuls of eggs into his mouth, and Miss Adele was eating the same oatmeal she ate every morning. She was smiling brightly. I had never seen her look so happy. I could tell she was overjoyed that her grandson was home. She obviously adored him, even if he did have issues. I picked at my eggs and took a bite of bacon.

"Do you like working here?" Edward asked as he sipped his coffee.

"I love it here," I answered honestly. "I've never been any place so beautiful. I don't know why you don't live here yourself. If I owned a house like this, I would never leave."

Edward threw his fork down on his plate and leaned forward and glared at me. I shrunk away from the intensity of his gaze.

He said. "This place has too many memories."

"Of your girlfriend?" I asked without thinking.

"Gossip spreads quickly here," he said without answering the question. Edward stood up and left the table. I looked over at Miss Adele. She seemed as happy as she had been a few minutes ago. She was eating her oatmeal with a large smile on her face. She seemed oblivious to the fact that I had just made her grandson so mad he'd stormed away from the table. I took a few bites of toast and finished my tea, not wanting to leave Miss Adele until she'd finished her breakfast.

After breakfast, I went to my room and tried to hide from the world. It was Saturday and I had to get through the rest of the weekend before I could escape back to school. I spent the rest of the morning studying, burying myself in my work. My course load was heavy and I was determined to graduate a year early, so I couldn't afford to fall behind. Once I graduated I could apply to med school, do my residency, and then I could begin working as an Emergency Room doctor. That was where my parents had dumped me when I was four years old. In the ER. That was where I wanted to make a difference.

A maid knocked on my door to tell me lunch was ready. I didn't want to go down to the dining room, again, and have to sit with Edward. I had no idea how to talk to him. He made me nervous and flustered, and it was all I could do not to blush every time he looked at me. The maid was nice enough to bring me back a sandwich when I told her I had to study.

After I ate, I decided to go out for a walk. It had become my usual routine. I would spend weekend mornings studying, but I would enjoy nice long walks in the afternoons. I'd thought about visiting Helen, but I didn't want to have to explain to her why I hadn't texted her since we'd arrived. I didn't want to have to ask her why she hadn't bothered to text me, either. And I didn't want to tell her about Edward. I knew what she would say. She would tell me to leave Thornfield, that I had already made enough money to pay for the dorms, there was no reason for me to stay on. I could hear her lecturing me. But I didn't want to leave Thornfield. I loved it here. Even though I could hear weird laughter at night. Even though there was a fire. Even though Edward made me feel so awkward. I felt like Thornfield was where I was supposed to be.

I left the house and the bustling noises behind and I walked into the gardens and down a narrow path that passed by the stables. I walked the path all the time. It was perfectly situated to give me a view of the horses without giving James a view of me. The path faced the back of the stables, so it felt hidden. All the horses were in the pasture. I watched them for a while. They stood eating grass in the shade of the trees that towered above the pasture. Their tails swished lazily back and forth. I hadn't spent much time with animals. I hadn't even had a cat or a hamster as a child. I climbed over the fence and walked up to a tall, lean horse. It was black with a white spot on its forehead. I reached out and put my hand on the side of the animal. It didn't acknowledge me. It just kept eating grass. I smiled and ran my hand across the animal's soft coat.

A breeze rustled the leaves of the trees above me and the horse meandered away. I looked around at all the other horses. There must have been at least a dozen in the pasture. I wished I knew how to ride. I turned to walk back to Thornfield and ran directly into Edward. I jumped backward in surprise.

"You scared me!" I yelled with an uncharacteristic display of temper. "How long have you been standing there?"

He didn't answer me for a while. He just kept watching me. I took that moment to return his stare. He was limping, and his ankle was in a brace. He had bandages on his arms from the burns. There was an angry cut on his face. None of this mattered. He was still beautiful.

"I'm sorry," I said finally. "I shouldn't have lost my temper. You just startled me."

"You can ride one if you like," he said after a while.

I shook my head. "I don't know how to ride."

"I'll teach you," he said. It was more of a command than an offer. He bellowed something at James. I hadn't noticed James before, but he'd obviously been in the nearby barn doing something with the animals. James set about gathering up two horses and saddling them.

We walked into the stables. I wasn't sure if I was really going to be brave enough to get on a horse. It was one thing to read about riding. It was another thing to get on an animal and trust it with your life.

"The black horse you were with," Edward said. "It was my favorite when I was a kid. She's getting old now, but she was always my favorite."

"You must have loved growing up here," I commented. "I certainly would have."

"I was here until I was thirteen and then my parents sent me to a boarding school. I went to Cranbrook until I was seventeen, and now I'm at Yale. I didn't really grow up here. I spent my summers here."

"Even so, it must have been nice being here for the summers," I said, for lack of anything else better to say.

He nodded.

"What're you studying at school?" I asked.

"Business."

James brought us our horses and gave me a knowing smile. I didn't return it. Undaunted by my expression he tried to help me onto the animal. He grabbed my leg and tried to guide me into the stirrup. Edward stepped in between us and scowled at James. He skulked away and I took a breath of relief. Edward continued watching James with a frown.

"You like your business classes?" I asked, drawing his attention.

"Someone needs to run the family businesses. I have to know how," he said as he lifted me onto my horse.

I grasped onto the saddle in front of me for dear life. "I don't think I want to do this," I said and I tried to climb down off the horse.

Edward pushed me back on. "Don't worry. She's a gentle girl. You'll be fine. Her name is Bella. Just pet her. She'll take care of you. I promise."

I clung to the horse and told myself it would be okay. People rode horses all the time and not all of them ended up in wheelchairs or dead. Edward got on his brown horse with confidence and ease. His limp didn't seem to stop him at all. His horse was much more spirited than mine and he had to reign it in a little to keep it from running away with him. Bella just lowered her head and began to eat grass.

"Are you OK? You are hurt? Should you be riding?" I wasn't sure if I was asking because I wanted to avoid riding or if I was genuinely concerned.

"It's just a sprain," he answered with a grin. "I'll be fine."

Edward whistled to Bella and we took off at a very slow pace into the woods. Bella was very responsive to Edward's whistles and clucks, and I hardly had to do anything at all to get her to stay on the path. I began to feel more at ease and I had to admit that it was an amazing feeling being on the back of a horse. The woods behind Thornfield were breathtaking. I smiled stupidly and stroked Bella's neck. It was a beautiful day and little purple wildflowers dotted the path. Birds sang in the trees above us and a gentle breeze cut through the lingering September heat. Edward looked back at me and smiled. That same smile from last night. He was dazzling when he smiled. I almost fell off the horse. He reached out and helped me regain my balance.

"You have to use your thighs to hold onto the horse," he explained. "You're sliding all over the place because you aren't holding on with your thighs."

I nodded and gripped the horse as tightly as I could with my legs. My butt hurt already.

"What classes are you taking?" he asked.

"I'm taking Organic Chemistry, Physics, Genetics, and Calculus and for my electives, English 102 and French."

"You seem to have skipped some classes. I thought you said you were only taking core classes. Those sound like higher level classes," he commented. "Don't you usually have to take Chemistry and Biology 101 before you get into the higher levels?"

"I took all of those in high school. I took AP Chemistry, Biology, English, European and U.S. History, and Government in high school," I said hesitantly. I hated admitting what a dork I was. "I'm hoping to graduate a year early," I added.

"So, you're hoping to graduate by the time you're nineteen? Do you ever sleep?"

I laughed. "I guess I am a workaholic. When do you graduate?"

"The same year as you, I guess, but I'll be an old man by then."

I laughed again. "Ancient. You'll need dentures. How old will you be?"

"Twenty-two. Like normal non-super humans who go to college."

"I am normal. I just like school."

We rode for a long time. Edward wasn't great with conversation, but then again, neither was I. Sometimes I would catch him looking back at me, but he seemed to be at a loss for words. We rode up the small mountain behind Thornfield and when we got to the top, he helped me off Bella. There was a tower on top of the mountain. It looked so run down that it was a wonder it was still standing. An odd-looking wooden hut sat at its top. I recognized what it was. It was a fire tower. I knew their history, but I had never seen one up close. In the early 1900s, people, called fire watches, were stationed in remote areas to keep a lookout for fires. They lived in fire towers and the towers were put on mountains so they could see smoke at a great distance. Most of the towers had fallen into disrepair and this one was no exception.

I glanced around. I wished there was a clearing because I imagined the view from the mountain top would have been spectacular if it weren't for all the trees. I had never really been in the woods. I had never been hiking or been on the top of a mountain. All these things were new to me. Sitting in the woods watching Edward tie up the horses, I realized that I had lived most of my life through books and movies. Every mountain I had seen was on the Discovery Channel or on the Internet. Every horse I had seen was on Animal Planet. This was the first time I had ever done something really adventurous.

Edward came over to me and took my hand.

"Where are we going?" I asked in dismay. For some reason, the stupid gossip about Edward flashed through my mind. I was in the middle of the woods, alone with Edward Rochester, who everyone thought was a murderer.

"I want to show you something."

CH∧PTER 11

I have harnessed the shadows that stride from world to world to sow death and madness.

~ H.P. Lovecraft

I SHOCK MY HEAD. I could see where he was taking me. He was taking me up the tall rusty, iron fire tower on top of the mountain, and there was no way I was climbing up that rickety structure. If he didn't kill me, I would probably fall and kill myself.

"You'll love it," he said. "I promise."

"How do you know I'll love it? You hardly know me. I can't climb that thing."

"I know you're a girl who spends her nights wandering lonely roads alone and bewitching horses. I know you are brave enough to walk through fire to save someone you hardly know. I know you love books about adventures and that you are kind to old ladies when you don't have to be. You smell of wildflowers, and even when there is nothing but anger and rage in my heart, when I am around you I become calm. I think I know you very well and I know you are too brave to turn away from a real adventure when you are offered one."

I laughed and blushed. My fear melted away in the face of so many compliments. "You think much too highly of me. I'm just an average girl and I've never climbed anything in my life. What if I fall?"

"I'll catch you."

"You have a sprained ankle. What if you fall?"

"You will have to catch me."

So, I followed him up the tower. I clung to the metal handrail and walked gingerly up the rotting steps, hoping that our combined weight wouldn't cause the stairway to crumble. When we got to the top, Edward opened the hatch to the wooden hut and we climbed in. Inside, the hut was filled with things that spoke of childhood. There were little plastic soldiers on the window sills and an old puzzle was spread out on a wooden table. Old blankets were tangled with cobwebs in the corners.

I walked over to the window and looked through the cobwebs and dust at a view that, literally, took my breath away. Tears filled my eyes. I had never imagined I would ever see this kind of beauty in my life. I could see for miles. The entire valley, in all its wonder, lay at my feet. Everything was green and beautiful. A breathtaking landscape that only Mother Nature could paint.

"Thank you," I said.

"I used to ride up here on Bella when I was a kid. This was my favorite place in the world."

"Why did you bring me here?"

"Because you saved my life and because I like you."

He stood behind me. He was so close I could almost feel him. Part of me wanted to be brave. Part of me wanted to turn around and pull him to me and kiss him like I imagined Helen kissed Jake. But I wasn't like Helen, so I walked away from him. I walked to the other window and looked out at the setting sun.

"We should go," I said. "It's getting late."

We rode back in complete silence. The sun set and the stars came out. The moon illuminated our path, but I didn't think the light was even necessary. The horses knew the way back to the stables so well they could have made the trip in their sleep. James came out to greet us when we arrived at the stables. Edward helped me off my horse and then he wandered back to Thornfield Hall alone. There was no invitation for me to come with him. He didn't invite me to eat dinner with him and Miss Adele that night. There were so many servants everyone decided to find their own meal and I was left to eat a sandwich alone in my room and wonder at my time spent with Edward. Why had he been so nice to me and then left me to walk back to the house alone? I don't think I would ever understand guys. Especially complicated guys like Edward.

CHAPTER 12

The most merciful thing in the world, I think, is the inability of the human mind to correlate all of its contents.

~ H.P. Lovecraft

I COULDN'T SLEEP AGAIN THAT night. I had so much on my mind I could barely lie still. I tried not to think about Edward, but whenever I stopped thinking about him I got nervous about my upcoming Calculus test on Monday and then I would try not to think about that and I would find myself thinking about Edward, again. The house was quiet. All the staff had gone for the night. It was just the three of us. And since I couldn't sleep, I got out of bed and wandered back to the tower room.

I climbed the winding staircase and picked up the old journal I'd dropped the night before. I sat on the bed and flipped through the pages. Whoever had put the journal together was more of an artist than a writer. It was filled with sketches. Most of them were of Edward. I found myself lingering over those pages the longest. I studied the shape of his nose and curve of his neck. The other drawings were of different places in Thornfield Hall. Whoever had drawn the pictures was a girl. I knew it. She drew the mansion, itself, and the gardens. There was even a picture of old Bella and Mrs. Fairfax. I found some photographs stuffed in the back of the sketchbook. I looked at the first one. It was a picture of a little girl sitting in an old rocking chair. The girl seemed mad. I moved to the next photograph. It was of a family. There were two angry looking parents and one sad little boy. This family made my childhood look happy and joyful. I had never seen a more miserable looking family photograph.

I flipped to the next photograph and it almost slipped from my fingers. I almost cried out in shock. It was a photograph of Edward and a beautiful girl. He looked so young in the photograph, it seemed almost criminal that he should have been dating. He couldn't have been more than fifteen or sixteen. He was smiling. He looked happy. I hadn't seen him look so happy. The girl next to him looked happy, too. She was also young and so pretty it hurt to look at her. She was a flower. She was a rose. Her hair was bright red and long. Her fair skin looked like ivory in her white gown. Her green eyes were like the grass on a summer day. She looked like a doll. The kind of doll that I had always wanted when I was a kid, but could never afford to have. I felt a pang of what I knew was jealousy. He had dated a great beauty. He had been so happy then. I knew that his parents had died when he was young, but what had happened to this girl? I tried to suppress thoughts of the horrible story the boy at the party had told me. I wouldn't believe Edward cut her up and set her on fire. But was she still around? Had she died, too, or did she break his heart and leave? How hard it must be to lose someone you love and only have your memories of them. Were those memories a comfort or a burden? I couldn't remember my own parents. They dumped me at the hospital when I was only four years old. But I had my own burden that I literally carried on my back. The tattoo that reminded me of where I'd come from and what kind of people my parents had been.

I slipped the journal into my pocket and wandered back downstairs. I was feeling quite depressed and didn't really think I was going to be able to sleep at all. I decided to visit the library and do some reading when I found Miss Adele standing in the middle of the hall, again.

She was looking out into the darkness of the hallway. I stood beside her and tried to make out what she was seeing, but there was clearly nothing there. I put my hand on her shoulder. She was shaking. There were tears in her eyes.

"I thought if he came back, he could forgive me. He could forgive us, but he never will. He'll never forgive us. He hates us." She wept.

"No one hates you, Miss Adele," I said reassuringly. "Who could possibly hate you?"

"Edward hates me. He hates us, but it wasn't our fault. It was the curse. It was the curse. We had to do it. We had to do it, or we would lose everything." Miss Adele was muttering. Tears streamed down her face.

I ran back to my room and got Miss Adele's valium and walked her carefully back to her room. I helped her into her bed and crushed the valium up into a cup of tea I'd brewed with the electric kettle on her dresser. She sat on her bed sobbing. I handed Miss Adele her tea and she drank it without question. It was green tea and it smelled of honey and jasmine. The aroma filled the room and surrounded Miss Adele. Slowly, her tears faded and she looked up at me with eyes thick with sleep.

"Be careful," she whispered to me. "You won't be the first girl to die for loving him. This family is cursed."

"There are no curses," I said as I stroked her hair. "There are no ghosts. Edward loves you. He came back to see you."

"He only came back because he had to. He only came back because of his duty. Don't you see? It will all crumble and burn if he doesn't do his duty."

Her eyelids grew heavy. The tea wrapped her in its valium-saturated arms and pulled her down. I tucked the covers up to her chin and wiped the tears from her eyes. The teacup was still warm. I looked at the tea leaves in the bottom of the cup. They had clumped together to form a kind of phantom face in the white china. I swirled the tea and the face vanished. Miss Adele snored and I put the cup down beside her.

I finally felt sleep calling to me, so I went back to my room instead of heading down to the library. I hoped that there wouldn't be any more phantom laughter to keep me up at night.

CH/\PTER 13

We live on a placid island of ignorance in the midst of black seas of the infinity, and it was not meant that we should voyage far.

~ H.P. Lovecraft

HELEN WAS WAITING FOR ME in the library of Thornfield Hall Monday morning. I had kept to myself all day Sunday, staying in my room studying for my test. I had only ventured out to the kitchen to grab something to eat when I was hungry and then to sit with Miss Adele until she fell asleep. Luckily, she'd slept through the night. I didn't cross paths with Edward again. He must have been avoiding me, too, because he didn't send a maid to invite me to eat with them or go riding. It didn't matter because I had to focus on my upcoming Calculus test.

Helen was all smiles when I stepped into the library. Her hair had changed color, again. It was a bright magenta. She was wearing skinny purple jeans with a glittery stripe down the side seam and a purple tank top that looked like lingerie. No one could dress like Helen and get away with it. She wrapped her arms around me and hugged me when she saw me.

"I thought you were going crazy," Helen said as she led me out of the library. "But it all makes sense now."

I knew I was in trouble. Whenever Helen said that things made sense, I was in trouble. "What makes sense?"

"I know why you only go to class and spend all your free time here. He's smoking hot. I saw him in his study. I was wondering why you hadn't climbed out the window of this place and why you hadn't texted me, but I don't blame you at all. That is the best-looking guy I have ever seen. Why didn't you tell me?"

"No!" I protested. "That isn't it at all. He just got here a couple of days ago and he's way too old for me and he isn't my type. He's moody and rude and kind of stuck up, to be honest."

"Oh my God!" Helen exclaimed. "You're falling for him! And he isn't too old for you. He looks like he's nineteen. That's only three years older than you."

"I'm not falling for him. I hardly know him." I stopped and looked at Helen. "He is nineteen and that is too old for me. I'm only sixteen. Either way, I don't have time to date. I have more important things to worry about."

Helen smiled a knowing grin. "Oh, stop! He is not too old for you. And I can tell how you feel about him. It's written all over your face."

I shook my head in protestation. "It doesn't matter if he's exactly my age or even six months younger. Guys like Edward aren't interested in girls like me and I have more important things to worry about. He's clearly got issues and I don't like to get involved in other people's issues."

Helen laughed. "You don't like to get involved in other people's issues? I love you like my sister, and part of the reason I love you is because you've been there for me, holding my hand through all my crazy issues. I'm a bag full of cats of crazy issues, and you know it. And I'm the only friend you have. You love getting involved in other people's issues. You want to be a doctor, for God's sake!"

I laughed. "Okay. So maybe you're right, but guys like that still don't want to have anything to do with girls like me."

Helen threw up her arms in frustration. "We have got to do something about your self-esteem problem. You're not a troll. You're different looking. And you're beautiful. You need to stop dressing like a bag lady and put on some make-up so everyone can see how uniquely beautiful you are.

I shook my head. "I'm not a troll, but maybe I'm some kind of lesser goblin." Helen rolled her eyes at me. "I've certainly never attracted attention from guys I actually liked. I only attract guys like James. I think he's half-troll and that is probably why he likes me. The only reason Edward talks to me is because I saved his life."

Helen laughed. "When you're all grown up you're going to be stunning and every guy you meet will fall at your feet. Trust me. And what are you talking about? You saved Edward's life?"

"He caught on fire."

"What?! When?! You've got to tell me everything."

I began telling Helen what had happened since I'd arrived. I let everything flow out of me like a river. I told her all the details. I told her about the fire that almost killed Edward and our magical ride to the fire tower. I even talked about the weird laughter that filled the house at night and Miss Adele's nocturnal wanderings. By the time I was done with my story, it was time for me to leave for class and Helen was looking at me as if she was mesmerized.

"He's in love with you, too," she said.

"We should walk to school together," I said, ignoring her comment.

"I can't," Helen answered with a strange half smile.

"Why not?"

"Just get your books and I'll explain when you get back."

I went up to my room, grabbed my things, but when I returned to the library Helen was gone. I sighed and made my way to class. Helen did that sometimes, showed up and then split on me. Sometimes I thought she might be embarrassed to be seen with me. She was cool and I was not. I didn't even know if it was cool to say cool anymore. I wondered what she'd wanted to tell me and why she'd disappeared. I hadn't seen her on campus since school started and we didn't have any classes together. I wondered if she'd ended up getting a job and decided to put school on hold. After all, she was living with her boyfriend. Maybe they were having too much fun living together and working and didn't feel like going to school? Helen had always been a mystery to me, but I loved her. She was like family. Not by blood, but by love.

CHAPTER 14

There is beauty in everything. Even in the silence and the darkness.

~ Helen Keller

I HAD TROUBLE CONCENTRATING THAT day. My mind kept wandering, jumping from Edward to Miss Adele to Helen. I maintained my focus well enough to ace my Calculus test, but I kept drifting away in Genetics. I quietly chastised myself for my silly thoughts, especially regarding Edward, so I went to the university library after class to study. I had cleared my mind almost entirely by the time I left to walk home.

By the time I returned to Thornfield, I was feeling better, more clear-headed. Overall, I was doing really well in my first semester and I was determined to graduate early and get my professional life off to a great start. I walked into the study and found Edward reading there. He was sitting behind the huge mahogany desk and looked beautiful with his nose in a book. His dark hair was kind of mussed like he'd been running his fingers through it while he was reading. He was dressed casually, in faded jeans and a Doctor Who t-shirt. Helen was right, he was probably only about nineteen. Helen's words had encouraged me to do something I wouldn't have done before.

"Can I join you and Miss Adele in the dining room tonight?" I asked boldly.

Edward put his book down and looked at me with more than a little bewilderment. "Of course," he answered.

I turned to leave. I didn't want to say something stupid that would undermine myself.

"Jane." Edward's voice stopped me dead in my tracks. All the boldness I had a few moments ago melted into a puddle at my feet and I trembled as I turned around to meet Edward's blue eyes. He was scowling and looking at me with his usual intensity.

"Yes?" I replied with a hint of a question in my voice.

"Stay with me a while," he said. "Sometimes I hear ghosts when I sit too long in this house by myself."

I stood still and listened for a moment. It was quiet. I had been so focused on classes and Helen's odd morning visit that I hadn't even noticed that the bustling staff had vanished. The house was clean and disturbingly silent. Even the regular staff was gone.

"Ghosts?" I asked, raising my eyebrows.

"I just meant that old houses make strange noises and this old house makes more than most."

I nodded and sat down across from him. He continued to stare at me as though he were dissecting my face, and it made me feel awkward. I wondered what he was thinking? Did he think I was cute or even pretty? My many walks in the warm summer sun had left highlights in my hair. I kind of liked it. My skin had also benefitted from the sun, good food, and long walks. I liked my skin better when it was darker from the sun. It seemed smoother and less blotchy. I had put on eyeliner that morning and my long curly brown hair was loose and down. I was wearing a pretty, red tunic that I had bought at a thrift store. It fit me well and had a low V-neck that gave a curvier look to my chest. I was wearing it with a pair of black leggings. I thought I looked nice, but who knows if Edward thought so; his eyes had that intense look in them again. He could have been angry or disgusted. I had no idea. I wasn't good at reading a guy's mind. I felt pretty insecure about myself in the best of times, and I assumed that no guy would ever be attracted to me. I felt awkward at the silence. I cleared my throat and said, "I just wanted to say thank you for the ride the other day. It was wonderful and I don't think I thanked you."

"I enjoyed it, too." Edward smiled just a little.

Silence filled the room and I looked around. Edward's study was filled with the types of things you imagined would be in a Victorian gentleman's study. It was kind of weird that he liked old stuff. I did, too, but I already knew I was weird. A collection of antique spyglasses sat on the huge mantel of the huge fireplace and a huge oil painting of a ship in a sea storm hung above it. Most of the rooms at Thornfield had a huge fireplace, probably dating back to when it was first built. I remembered what Mrs. Fairfax said about fires, but there were no papers or books near the fireplace.

Two large burgundy leather club chairs were angled toward the fireplace and bookshelves lined an entire wall. Thornfield was full of books. That, alone, made me happy. There was no computer. All the things that would be found in a modern study were conspicuously absent. I felt like I had slipped back in time. Even Edward seemed oddly out of time, too. In the wrong era. Was it such a bad thing to feel out of place in your own time?

"Do you play chess?" he asked abruptly.

"Y-yes, but not very well," I replied evasively.

"Will you play with me?"

"Okay," I said. We moved over to the back corner of the study. It was dark and had two smaller leather chairs and an antique glass top table between them. The glass top was actually a built-in chess board and the pieces were laid out. I settled down in one of the leather chairs and looked at the board nervously. I'd lied to Edward. I was actually very good at chess. I didn't own up to it because it was another one of those things that made me stand out as a weirdo in school. I had won several chess tournaments and was considered the best player on my chess team in high school. Of course, I was a dork even by chess team standards, which probably made me the queen of dorks. I hesitated before I made my first move. I wondered what Helen would advise. Should I play honestly or let him win? It seemed unethical to let him win, so I played like I always played.

We moved through the game quickly. Edward was a decisive player and he wasn't bad, but by the time we made it to the middle of the game I had a distinct advantage.

"Did you tell me you weren't good at chess because you didn't want to play with me or because you are ridiculously humble?" he asked as he moved his queen to the center of the board.

I studied the board. "I don't know," I said honestly. "Being good at chess has never really won me any friends, so I never admit to it. I love chess, but it's one of those things girls aren't supposed to be good at."

"Do you hide all your skills or is this it?" he said. "Should I worry about you having an arsenal of superpowers I know nothing about?"

I laughed. "You never know."

Edward looked up at me and smiled. "I think you are hiding more about yourself. You and I are a lot alike. I've spent my entire life hiding. You shouldn't hide who you are to make other people happy."

I moved my bishop and leaned back in my chair. "It really doesn't matter if I hide who I am," I commented. "I'll never be one of the popular girls, anyway."

Edward scowled as he studied the board. "You're out of high school now. You don't have to worry about things like that anymore."

I smiled. "I keep forgetting that. It is different here. I don't feel quite so out of place. I even look forward to going to school."

Edward moved his rook and then he leaned back to study me. I really wished he would stop doing that. I tried to focus on the game and avoid making eye contact.

"Why do you want to be a doctor?" he asked.

I couldn't help smiling. "I want to help people." I put up my hand before he could say anything. "I know. I know. I've read a hundred books and they all say you're not supposed to say that on your med school interviews, but for me it's the truth. I want to be a doctor because I want to help people. I know it's stupid and cliché, but I read this book called Where There Are No Doctors. It was a true story about a physician who went to Africa to work with people who are super poor and dying of things that could be cured with antibiotics. It just seemed like such an amazing thing, to be able to really save and change someone's life like that. Ever since then, I knew I wanted to be a doctor." I didn't tell him about the other reason. About the doctor who saved my life when I was only four years old and had developed a terrible infection from the tattoo cut into my back in some hellish ritual I was fortunate enough to have forgotten. My case managers had made of point of telling me the story over the years. I had heard it so many times, I felt like I could remember it if I tried. I never tried.

I moved my knight. "Check," I said.

Edward didn't look at the board. He just kept looking at me. "Well, I'm not as noble as you. I'm fairly sure there aren't many people as noble as you, but I wanted to study English and be a professor. I like to read and I like school. It was always my favorite place. I envy you and your chance to follow your dreams. I have to study what I am told to. I have to run the family business."

Our eyes met and I held his gaze. "Why don't you follow your dreams? You're not hurting for money. You seem to be smart enough. Why not just study what you want to?"

This time it was Edward whose gaze skittered away. He looked back down at the chess board and studied the pieces. "My family has always been complicated. I have to meet my family obligations."

"What are those?"

"I have to go to the right school, take the right classes, date the right girls." He seemed so bitter and angry, I could almost feel his rage.

"Are you kidding me? What is this? The 18th century? I'm certainly not rich and I'm telling you, right now, I wouldn't give up the chance to live my dream for all the money in the world!" My hands shook with passion as I spoke.

"I wish it were that easy," he said. He moved his queen to protect his king. "My family is old. We're so old, we had this house moved from England in the 18th century. We used to be aristocrats. There are things we just have to do. Things we'll always have to do. It isn't just an obligation to us. I am different. All of the men in my family are."

"Different?" I asked.

"It's complicated. I would say you wouldn't understand, but I think you might be the only person who would. There is something about you, Jane Marsh... I can't put my finger on it. Either way, trust me when I tell you that I have to do as I am told. Bad things happen when I don't."

"Bad things?"

"People die when a Rochester breaks the rules. Haven't you heard the stories? The ghosts of the dead haunt this house still."

I couldn't tell if he was joking, but he seemed kind of scary in that moment. I leaned back from him a little.

Edward just shook his head. "Tell me more about what you are studying at school."

I took his queen with my knight. "Checkmate."

He grinned at that. "Shit. You are good."

I shrugged my shoulders and grinned back. "Well, like I mentioned the other day, I'm taking all the usual pre-med courses, but I do love my English class. We're reading *100 Years of Solitude*. It is so good. I also love Organic Chemistry more than any normal girl should."

"You keep saying that. Why would you want to be a normal girl? I know lots of normal girls. They're all boring. There's nothing wrong with being different. Be yourself, Jane. Be the witchy girl I found wandering alone in the woods at night who walked through fire to save me. Be the girl who is smarter than everyone else in the room. Don't let anyone else tell you who you should be." He picked up his fallen king and held it tightly.

I arched an eyebrow and looked at him. "This from a guy who has to do as he's told? When will you be who you are?"

"I'm having some friends here this week," he said, obviously changing the subject. "I'm having a party. Would you stay for my party on Friday?"

I blushed and looked down at the chess board again. "I don't do well at parties."

With the chess game over, he had nothing to do but stare at me again. "Have you been to many parties?"

"I went to one last week," I said. I kept looking at the board.

"How do you know you don't do well at parties if you've only been to one party?"

I got up and walked across the room and sat in one of the chairs by the fireplace." Because I don't do well in large groups."

Edward followed me across the room, but he didn't sit down. "We should go to dinner." He extended his hand to me. I looked at it for a minute before I finally accepted. I expected him to let go of my hand once he helped me to my feet, but he held on and led me to the door. I allowed him to pull me down the hall toward the dining room. Before we got to the room, he stopped and just held onto my hand. He drew me close to him. I could feel his body against mine. I couldn't even remember ever being that close to another human being. I trembled as he put his other hand on my shoulder. I looked up at him and saw something in his eyes that made me want to hold onto his hand forever. It terrified me. I let go of his hand and stepped back.

"Come to my party." His pleasant request had turned into an order. "I need someone there to keep an eye on my grandmother and her nurse leaves at eight."

"Of course," I whispered. He was my boss and watching over his grandmother was my job. I couldn't say no.

CHPTER 15

"Light is easy to love. Show me your darkness."

~ R. Queen

JENNA WAS THE ONLY SERVANT that night at dinner. The rest of the staff had left early. She served us dinner and I ended up helping her when she seemed overwhelmed by the chore. Sitting down while someone else struggled with their work just seemed wrong. She smiled at me and thanked me for my help. As we filled the soup bowls in the kitchen to carry out to the dining room, she stepped closer to me. "Be careful." She whispered so softly I almost didn't hear her.

I wanted to ask her what she meant. I wanted her to tell me more, but Miss Adele's nurse came into the kitchen to get a cup of tea for her. And then the moment was gone.

Miss Adele seemed even more out of sorts than usual. Her hair was disheveled and she had a wild look in her eyes. She seemed afraid. The nurse had to feed her the soup. Miss Adele waved her away causing the soup to spill on the hardwood floor. The sound echoed in the empty house. I wasn't sure what to say to Edward. He was quiet and I didn't have the words to fill the void, so I went into the kitchen for a fresh bowl of soup and fed it to Miss Adele. The nurse should have done this but it looked like there was a Candy Crush crisis that was taking priority. I focused on my task. Miss Adele calmed down for me. She looked into my eyes and ate the soup. Her eyes became less wild and she even smiled a little.

I didn't eat much. I ate my soup and a little of the roast chicken, but I had enough butterflies in my stomach to fill a garden. Edward cleared his plate and had room for seconds. When dinner was over, Edward rose and walked across the long room and gave his grandmother a kiss on the cheek. He helped her up and Adele's nurse took her back to her room. Then he turned to me and offered me his hand again. I was surprised that he did because of my earlier reaction. But I surprised myself even more. I took it.

I closed my eyes and felt his skin on mine. His hand was warm and strong. His grasp was firm. I felt the way his fingers wrapped around mine like ivy clinging to a wall. That feeling came over me again, the feeling that made me want to hang onto his hand forever. He pulled me to my feet and stood facing me. I know he wanted me to look at him. I wanted to look at him, too, but it was too much. I got scared and looked away. He let go of my hand and walked out of the dining room, leaving me standing there feeling more alone than ever.

CHPTER 16

Ultimate horror often paralyses memory in a merciful way.

~ H.P. Lovecraft

I WOKE UP IN MY bed at 3 a.m. At first, I wasn't sure what it was that woke me, but I quickly realized that my door was open. I grabbed Miss Adele's valium and walked into the hall expecting to see her standing by the door. I assumed that she had opened my door looking for the solace I offered her in the middle of the night, but she was nowhere to be seen. I turned on the light and looked up and down the corridor. No one was there.

The light flickered and then went out, and a chill filled the hall. I wrapped my arms around myself and walked down the long, narrow corridor. What was going on? There had been at least 100 people here over the week, madly working and making sure the entire house was in ship-shape. Now the lights weren't working and it was cold? I walked to Miss Adele's room and went in to check on her. Just to make sure she was okay. She was sound asleep, looking cozy under her down-filled comforter. I went back out of the room. It was still dark and still chilly. I heard a noise and, turning, saw someone standing at the end of the hall. I froze. My feet were rooted to the floor. I couldn't move no matter how many times I told myself that ghosts were just a silly superstition, I couldn't stop my heart from racing in blind panic.

"Edward?" I called out. There was no answer, only silence.

I took a tentative step forward. My legs shook beneath me. I could hardly bring myself to take another step, but I forced myself. I told myself not to be a scaredy cat. I willed myself to move toward the shadowy figure standing in the darkness. It became so cold, I could see my breath in the air in front of me. The lights flickered on, again, just enough that I could see that it was a young woman in front of me. She was dressed in white and so thin she was little more than a wisp of light. She carried a single candle in her hand. She was lovely. Long dark hair framed a pale, heart-shaped face. Her velvety brown eyes were sad.

I stood, clutching myself in cold and terror, waiting for the phantom in front of me to do anything. I reached down and pinched my arm. I dug my fingernails into my arm. I tried to wake myself, but I definitely wasn't dreaming, and I was definitely completely wrong about my previous beliefs about ghosts. Ghosts were real and this pale lady in front of me was as much proof as I would ever need of that.

I began to back up slowly, but the ghost's pale hand reached out to me and my legs gave out beneath me. I fell to the ground and sat in stunned silence. I was paralyzed with fear.

"Jane," the ghost whispered. "I knew he would bring you back to me."

I answered without thought. "Who?"

The ghost smiled and my blood ran cold. "You are beautiful. He told me you were beautiful. I am so glad you are here."

I was too scared to respond, so I just sat on the floor staring up at the ghost. She turned from me and pointed toward a locked door and then she was gone. It was as if she had never been there, at all. The warmth returned to the hall and the lights grew bright again. It was like nothing happened. I looked around and wondered if I hadn't been sleepwalking. I pulled myself to my feet and tried to tell myself it was a waking dream. It wasn't real. It couldn't have been real. I was overtired and overstressed, and it couldn't have been real. I stumbled back to my room and for the first time since I had been at Thornfield, I locked the door.

I slept fitfully and morning came too soon. The sun blinded me with its cruel fingers and pulled me out of bed. I didn't shower. I just threw on my shorts and a t-shirt and stumbled back into the hall. In the bright light of day, the hallway seemed like it always did. It was hard to imagine being scared of something with the morning birds singing and the sun dancing on the walls. I wandered the hall in the quiet of the early morning, searching for any evidence of something that could explain what had happened to me the night before. I studied the walls and the carpets.

I looked for windows and cameras. I tried to find a way to tell myself that it was all a practical joke, but I couldn't find any evidence that anyone had been in the house except Miss Adele, Edward, and me. I knew Miss Adele wasn't capable of pulling off an elaborate hoax and Edward just didn't seem like the type to pull a prank on anyone.

Finally, I found my way back to the locked door the ghost had pointed to. Why had she pointed to the door? What did she want me to know? I ran to Mrs. Fairfax's office and found a set of keys. I didn't like stealing, but I told myself it wasn't actually stealing, it was only borrowing, and I would return them after. I opened the door and it groaned angrily. It had probably been decades since it had been opened.

Behind the door there was only stairs and darkness. There were no light switches. There were no signs that the modern world had touched this part of the house, at all. I had to use my cell phone to cast a weak beam of light into the darkness, so I could see where I was going. The stairs were made of stone and looked so old they could have been in a medieval fortress. Cobwebs filled the corners and spiders crawled on the walls. I took a deep breath and stepped into the darkness. The door groaned shut behind me.

CHAPTER 17

I could not help feeling that they were evil things—mountains of madness whose farther slopes looked out over some accursed ultimate abyss.

~ H.P. Lovecraft

I WANTED TO JUMP BACK into the safety of the hall, but curiosity pulled me forward with as much tenacity as any emotion I had ever known. I climbed the stone steps, slowly. My feet were still bare and the cold stone was so frigid beneath my feet it sent a shiver up my spine. The air around me was stale and stuffy. It smelled of dust and I coughed and placed my hand over my mouth. When I made it to the top of the stairs, I found myself in an attic so immense it could have been a gymnasium.

The stone steps gave way to a wooden floor. The wood was soft with age and green with mold. Light filtered in through old glass windows cut into the stone walls. All around me were centuries of artifacts that the Rochester family must have brought with them from England when they migrated. I wondered if anyone even knew that these things were up here. Did Edward know? There were old suits of armor and piles of swords. Taxidermized animals stared out at me with glass eyes. There were paintings of long dead lords and ladies half covered in burlap. I wiped the decades of dust off the faded oil canvases to study the faces. Nobody ever smiled in paintings back then. The dead eyes of Edward's ancestors stared out at me, coldly. I could almost hear them whispering that I didn't belong in Thornfield Hall. I walked deeper into the attic, pushing cobwebs out of my way as I went. I found old cribs and bassinets. Creepy china dolls, wearing moldy dresses, sat on very old furniture.

Trying to find whatever the ghost had wanted me to see in this attic would be like trying to find a needle in a haystack. An impossible task. A spider scurried across my bare foot and I yelped, shaking it off. I lost my balance and tumbled into a pile of old blankets. Bugs scurried out in every direction and I jumped up frantically trying to dust them off me.

My phone rang and I almost fell back into the bug covered blankets again. I regretted my ringtone a little at that moment. I don't know what I could possibly have been thinking when I chose the theme song to The Shining. I had always loved Stephen King, but the music almost made me faint as the bugs danced over my bare feet.

"Crap," I muttered to myself as I juggled my cell phone. I answered my phone with a grumbling hello.

"How'd it go?" It was Helen. Of course, it was Helen. "Did you go to dinner with Edward?"

"I did," I said as I stared at the most disturbing stuffed bunny I had ever seen. Who'd made these children's toys? They looked like they were made by the same guy who designed Chucky.

"Well? Tell me everything!" she said.

"You know, for someone who acts like a rebel and a punk, you really are an incurable romantic," I commented.

"Hey! I resent that." She paused for a minute. "No. That is definitely true and I don't resent it at all. I want you to be happy like Jake and I are happy. I'm tired of seeing you alone with nothing but a book to keep you company. I have never seen you light up for anything the way you light up when I mention Edward."

Something fell over in the distance. A thud echoed throughout the attic. I turned to find the noise. A bird had found its way into the room and it sat perched on an old bit of armor. I didn't know my ornithology, but it looked like a raven or a crow. The raven looked at me and cawed and then it flew toward the back of the attic. I followed the bird into the darkness.

"Are you listening to me?" Helen's voice seemed a thousand miles away.

"Yes, how are you and Jake doing?" I asked.

The raven had flown to the back of the attic where a large wooden chest sat buried beneath a pile of ancient clothes. It flew up to the rafters above me and watched as I pushed the old clothes off the chest. I could hear Helen talking on the other end of the line, but I couldn't focus on her words. I dropped the phone. One lonely window sat above the old chest, casting just enough light for me to see. I opened the chest, carefully. It was so old I was afraid it would turn to dust in my hands. The hinges moaned and the chest revealed mountains of letters tied together with ribbons. I looked up, but the bird was gone. It had flown away. This is what I was meant to find. I knew it. I looked around and found an old bag, filled it with the letters, and closed the chest. I grabbed my phone and scampered out of the attic, coughing as I went.

CHAPTER 18

The moon is dark, and the gods dance in the night; there is terror in the sky, for upon the moon hath sunk an eclipse foretold in no books of men or of earth's gods.

~ H.P. Lovecraft

I SHUT THE ATTIC DOOR and ran down the hall just in time to bump into Edward. I slammed into him at such a velocity that I knocked myself off my feet. He caught me and helped me back up. I was breathless and feeling more than a little guilty about going someplace I knew I wasn't meant to be, so I just looked down at my feet and tried to avoid his gaze. I was filthy. Cobwebs were caught in my hair and my shirt was covered in dust. I knew I must have looked awful. I just wanted to get back to my room to hide the letters and take a shower.

"Did you decide to dust the guest rooms with your body?" Edward asked as he looked me up and down.

"No. I just got lost and fell down. It's a big house, you know? It's easy to get lost. I have to go shower." I turned and sprinted back to my room, slamming the door behind me. I locked the door and emptied my sack of letters onto the bed.

The letters were like a treasure to me. They weren't just treasure because of the ghost or because they were some kind of proof of the supernatural—although these things would have made them treasure enough—they were precious because my little geek mind loved the mystery of it all. These were first-hand accounts from a long dead time. They were real history. I was thrilled. I picked up the first stack of letters and carefully untied the old red ribbon that held them together. My hands shook as I undid the ribbon. I didn't even care that I was dirty anymore. I just wanted to know what was inside.

I took the first letter off the top of the stack. The paper was so old and so frail, I had to be careful to prevent it from crumbling. The ink was faded and the edges of the parchment were torn and tattered. I could barely read the words, but there was just enough ink left on the page for me to make them out.

August 12, 1692

My Beloved,
How I long to see you. My days are nothing but darkness without your embrace. Time travels like a ship, set out to drift upon a windless ocean when you are away from me. Every night I fall to my knees and pray for your safe return. I pray you will return to my

arms. As our wedding night draws closer, I am left only to dream of what joy I will find in the bliss of our wedding bed. My heart races with radiant joy to imagine what life will be like when I am your wife. Return to me quickly, my beloved, and put my suffering to an end. I can't bear another night without you.

Forever yours,
Liliana Lowood

I set the letter down, gingerly. I would have to do some research on how to preserve old paper. I would have to find out how to keep the letters safe so that I wouldn't be the only one to read them. The letters belonged in a museum. I smiled and brushed my fingers across the paper. I looked at the mountain of letters that were scattered across my bed. I was sure they would reveal a love story. Helen would be thrilled.

I suddenly realized that my phone had been ringing. I didn't know how long it had been ringing. I had been in a kind of trance. I picked up my phone and put it to my ear.

"What the hell? You hung up on me?" It was Helen again.

"Will you help me with a project?" I asked.

"What now? We were talking about Edward? What happened with Edward?"

I sighed. "You know I'm terrible with guys. I think I did everything wrong. He was wonderful. He held my hand and maybe he even wanted to kiss me, but I screwed it up.

Even if he was madly, insanely in love with me, I would find a way to mess this up. Guys make me nervous and I ruin everything."

"How did you screw up?"

"I don't know. He just makes me so nervous. I jumped away from him when he tried to kiss me. I sat as far away from him as I could and didn't talk to him during dinner. I don't think he likes me much anymore." I hoped he did still like me, but I had no way of knowing. I certainly couldn't ask him.

There was a silence on the other end of the phone and then Helen answered me. "I'm free this afternoon. What project do you want help with?"

"You're gonna love it!"

CHAPTER 19

We shall see that at which dogs howl in the dark, and that at which cats prick up their ears after midnight.

~ H. P. Lovecraft

HELEN WAS GOING TO JOIN me to go through the letters, but first I had to be sure I was taking proper care of them. I went to the university library and did some research about how to preserve old letters. I ended up spending more than I wanted on all the supplies I needed so that we could handle them and store them properly.

When I finally made it back to my room, Helen was waiting for me. She sat on my bed like she owned it. I had to wonder how Helen snuck into the house without anyone noticing her, but she seemed to have cat burglar skills that rivaled the best ninjas. Helen told me I was a geek at least five times when she saw the lengths to which I had gone to in order to protect the letters, and she also reminded me that I was an old lady trapped in a teenage girl's body. I laughed and made fun of her desperate need to find out who wrote the letters. For a minute, it was like old times. We were high school girls again. I missed those days when it was just me and Helen. Jake lived far away and our lives weren't complicated by guys and the messiness of relationships. I didn't miss being alone all the time at school or being made fun of, but I missed those precious moments at night when Helen snuck in my bedroom window and spent all night hanging out with me.

I had purchased everything we needed, so we were equipped with two pairs of cotton gloves and several scrapbooks with hard cardboard pages and clear plastic to keep the paper rigid and acid-free. I was thrilled. Helen was clearly excited, too. We put on our gloves, and Helen tore into the second letter and I yelled at her for being too rough. She slowed down and, once the first few letters were placed in plastic, Helen gave me a look just begging me to let her read it. So, we lay back on my enormous bed and started reading.

August 15, 1692

My Beloved,
You have left me adrift upon a foreign sea and only you can save me. I sit, day after day, waiting for your return. I wait with bated breath from any word from you, but you have abandoned me. I close my eyes and conjure images of you. I imagine you in your castle,

surrounded by all the great lords and ladies of the land. I wonder if some fair maiden has captured your eye and your heart. Perhaps that is why you have left me.

Life here continues on. My family sees my broken heart as the fancy of a foolish girl. I sit by the window with my mother and my sisters while we do our embroidery and listen to them speak of all the things that once ruled my life. They all seem so small now. They seem so far away. Diana, my eldest sister, is to be wed in a fortnight. Her bridegroom is a merchant from London. She likes him well enough, but I can't imagine marrying a man who doesn't set my heart on fire the way you do. Still, she seems happy enough and that pleases me for I have great affection for her and wish her all the happiness in the world.

Please send word, my beloved. The world has lost its color and my tears never end. Let me know you are still alive.

Forever yours,
Liliana

Helen picked up the next letter and carefully set it on the cardboard and covered it in plastic.

"Do you think they're all like this? Do you think she just pines away after this guy, year after year?" Helen asked. "I don't think I could bear that. I hope he falls off his horse and breaks his neck."

"I don't think so," I said as I opened another packet of letters. "This stack seems to be from a Richard Rochester IV."

August 14, 1692

My Darling,

I have finally arrived at my family's estate outside of Newcastle. It is so beautiful here. I can see you here at Thornfield Hall. Your lips are the same color as the roses in the gardens and your skin as delicate as the dew that clings to them in the mornings. I long to see you wandering the halls. My father assures me that we can be wed in the summer. We must settle affairs here before I can return to you. The estate here is in a terrible mess and my father says it would be wrong of me to marry before I set my affairs in order.

It is difficult for me to be as patient as my family dictates, however. The wind whispers your name and the nights are long and cold. I rode out onto the Moors last night and I thought I saw you standing in the shadows. There is a haunting quality to the landscape here that reminds me of you and your many ghost stories. You belong here, my love. Although time and space divide us, know you are always in my heart and I am yearning for the moment we can be together again.

Yours Always,
Richard Rochester.

Helen began to read the next letter in her packet.

October 1, 1692

My Beloved,
It has been many months since I have had the time to
write you. My sister's wedding has consumed all of our
time. I have spent my days working on her wedding
gown and helping her brew her bridal ale. The town
is alive with excitement. The party is sure to put all
others to shame. Yet even though my hours are spent
working toward my sister's shining moment, I cannot
stop thinking of you. I still await word from you. Have
you forgotten about me? Do you still love me at all?

The sun is setting as I write this letter and my
mother is calling to me. I am ignoring her words to
write in hopes that my words will somehow find their
way to your heart and bring you back to me.

Forever Yours,
Liliana

September 1, 1692

My Darling,
Since I last saw you, my fortune has failed me. I wish
you were here to ease my suffering with your soft lips.
Your words would take all my worry away. Our estate,

here, is in such a terrible state that we have had to sell some of our lands. My father has already sold several of our holdings in the South and he lectures me daily on my duties to my family. I know he wants me to forget you and the promises I made you to seek love in the arms of a woman with wealth and a handsome dowry, but I promise you that I will never forsake you. I am promised to you and I would rather be a pauper in your arms than a king in the arms of another.

Write to me, my love. I long to hear from you. I miss our simple lives in the country. I am alone here and time passes slowly in the fog. It seems that all there is here is loneliness and the knowledge that my family is falling apart around me. My mother says that my father has ruined us. She says he gambled our lives away, but I only know that I wish you were with me.

Always Yours,
Richard

The light flickered above us and Helen picked up another letter. "How long can it go on like this?" she asked as she read.

October 21, 1692

My Beloved,
My sister is wed now, and all are saying that she is already with child, although I think it is far too soon

to tell. She is a happy bride and her radiance fills every room she walks into. It also fills me with sorrow. I still haven't heard from you and I wonder if you are still mine, at all. Am I ever to be a bride? My parents want me to put you behind me. Your lands here are sold and they say you will never return. They tell me that I should meet with the other suitors who are eager to make me their bride, but I can't forget you. Where are you, my love? I fear if I don't hear from you soon I will be given to another.

I wandered the old castle today and thought of you. The ghosts there whisper your name. I think they remember us and our love. They wait for us. I have heard that witches used to live in the castle in the days of yore. Some call this place Witching Hill and say evil things wait here, but I fear nothing now. I only fear losing you. The witches that lived here were burned long ago, but their ghosts and their magic remain here. It is heresy to think this, but I wonder if their magic could bring you back to me. How I long to hold you! There is only sorrow for me now and ghosts.

Forever Yours,
Liliana.

I put another letter in the scrapbook and looked at the pile of papers on my bed. They weren't all letters. There was an old book and a journal. I opened one of the books. It was filled with handwritten notes. At first the notes looked like recipes, but upon careful study, they were spells.

"Look at this," I said to Helen.

Helen left her letters and took the journal. "This is just creepy. How did you find this stuff?"

I shrugged.

"How did you find this stuff?" Helen persisted.

"You were right," I said. "There is something supernatural here. I saw a ghost."

"Are you kidding me?" she exclaimed.

I shook my head.

"You saw a ghost?"

I nodded.

"And the ghost showed you these letters?"

I nodded again.

"We need to get you out of here. I've seen enough horror movies to know these things never end well. I told you not to stay here. I told you this place was creepy. You can quit tonight. You have enough money to stay in the dorms. They've paid you well. You've saved up enough."

"No!" I yelled. "I love it here."

"You love it in a haunted, probably cursed, castle? I'm weird, but I believe in self-preservation and it is time to think about preserving yourself and getting the hell out of here."

"I can't leave," I muttered.

"Because of him?"

"Maybe… but also because I've never been so happy as I've been here. There's a mystery here waiting to be solved and I can't go until I solve it." My eyes filled with tears and

I wiped them away. I must have been feeling all emotional because of the letters.

"I thought I was supposed to be the one who chased trouble," Helen said with a shake of her head.

"You're rubbing off on me." I sighed. It was true. I'd never felt more alive as I had at Thornfield.

Helen looked at the book of letters we'd made. She touched the old paper with her cotton glove. "You are the closest thing to a real family I've ever had," she said sadly. "My father still gives me nightmares. I still wake up afraid he might…" Her voice trailed off for a moment. "My mother is gone. Jake… Well, relationships can get complicated. I don't know what I'd do if something happened to you, Jane. You have to promise me you'll be sensible and safe."

"I'm always sensible and safe. You don't need to worry about me."

Helen laughed. "You're right."

I glanced out the window. It was dark. A sliver of a moon hung in the starry night sky.

Helen looked at her watch. "When did it get so late?" she asked.

As if on cue, the nurse popped her head in the room. "I'm heading out, now," she said. "Miss Adele is all tucked in."

"I'm in for the night," I said. "I'll check in on her later."

"I think I saw Edward go out for the night, so it's just you," she added.

"Thanks," I said.

"I'm spending the night," Helen said.

"You don't have to. I'm fine here. I'm not afraid of ghosts."

"Still, I can stay and we can work on more letters."
I smiled. "This one is dated December 1, 1692."

December 1, 1692

My Darling,
I wish you would write me and tell me you still love
me. I long to hear from you and I need to know you
are still there. I now know my parents moved us here
deliberately to get me away from you. I always knew
they opposed the match, but I didn't know how much
until recently. Over the last month, they have paraded
every eligible maid of good fortune through the house. It
has been made quite clear to me that the family's future
lies in my choice of wife. I have been true to you, my
darling. I have told them, again and again, that we
were promised to one another in front of God. What
God has put together no man may tear apart.

Their scorn and derision are unending and they
have made me a virtual prisoner here. They assure
me that you no longer love me. They say you have
found another. I can't believe them. I won't let myself
be undone by such blatant falsehoods, but without
word from you, I find myself wondering if there isn't
some seed of truth in what they say. Do you still love
me at all?

Always Yours,
Richard

December 5, 1692

My Beloved,
Where are you? I call out your name in the night and
there is no answer. As weeks have passed into months,
my desperation has grown into panic. I know that
you must have forgotten me and found some other
blushing bride of good family and fortune to fill your
bed. I conjure her image in my mind and it drives me
wild with anger and rage. My emotions pass through
me like a fog. Sometimes they fill me with such anger
that I think of doing unspeakable things. Other times
they fill me with such sorrow, I dream of ending my
own life. I have forgotten what you look like. I can
only remember your eyes, as blue as the ocean before
a storm.

My youngest sister, Martha, will be married
within a fortnight. Her bridegroom is an older man
with fortune enough to spare. Martha always was the
pretty one. Everyone is full of mirth and gaiety, but I
can hear them whisper of me. My family has given me
up for a spinster. They say my mind has been addled by
my love for you, but I can never touch another man.
You are my end and my beginning. There will never
be another.

At night, I wander the old ruins alone. I can
hear the witches of old speaking to me from their
graves. Sometimes, when the moon is lost in shadow,
darker things call out to me in the night. They make

me promises. Oh, my darling, I will make you mine again. I promise you will be mine.

Forever Yours,
Liliana.

Helen put the letter down. "Is it just me or is that kind of creepy?"

"Definitely," I answered. "We should go eat. It's late and no one is in the kitchen. We could go grab some sandwiches."

Helen and I ate in the kitchen and then I gave her a tour of the parts of Thornfield she hadn't seen yet, including the tower room and the attic. Helen always carried a flashlight with her, which helped a lot when we got to the attic. We wandered the house like we were ghosts ourselves. We tried to keep quiet and go unseen. I didn't want Edward to know I had a friend over. I wasn't even sure I was allowed to have friends over. We whispered as we walked and clung to the shadows. We didn't turn on lights, we just wandered in the dark.

Before we went to my room for the night, I peeked in on Miss Adele. She was sleeping soundly. When I came back to the room, Helen was sitting on my bed holding an old book in her hands. She'd put on the cotton gloves for me, but she had a sad look in her eyes.

"What is it?" I asked as I plopped down on the bed next to her.

"Liliana was burnt as a witch," Helen said.

CHAPTER 20

"Sometimes on feels that it would be merciful to tear down these houses, for they must often dream"

~ H.P. Lovecraft

"WHAT?"

Helen held out the old book. "These are legal records. The Rochester family accused her of witchcraft and had her burnt at the stake."

I put on my gloves and took the book from Helen. I didn't open it. I just looked at it.

"I guess that's one way to get rid of the poor girl your son is in love with," Helen said. "I'm so glad I didn't live back then. They would have burnt me for sure. Is there even any point in finishing the letters? We know what happens."

I carefully moved all the letters to my desk. I stacked them in a neat pile away from the window. "We can finish them later. I still want to read all of them. I also want to get them properly mounted for storage. There is a lot of history in those letters. I'm sure someone wants them preserved."

Helen stood up and got undressed. She pulled an old t-shirt on. She always slept in the same oversized shirt. It had a pink care bear on it. I don't know where she got it. She must have had it in her purse. I started to undress and put my nightgown on, but Helen grabbed me after I took my shirt off. I stood in front of her, topless, and I could tell something was wrong. She was staring at my back.

"What?" I asked with trepidation. Part of me knew why she was staring and I didn't want to hear it.

"Your tattoo… It looks different. Bigger."

I ran to the bathroom mirror and craned my neck to see my back. "Holy shit," I whispered as I stared at the reflection.

The tattoo had spread. Behind the door, an entire landscape had grown. There was a burning castle surrounded by ashes and decay. Skulls littered the grass in front of the door and tiny horned beasts hid in the skulls. Dark clouds filled the sky and the moon hung heavily in the inky black heavens. A solitary black cat sat in front of the door. A keyhole had appeared in the door and a red light shone from behind it. For a while, both Helen and I just stared at the massive piece of art. The tattoo was spreading and I could see bits of it wrapping around my ribs.

"What're you going to do?" Helen asked.

"I-I don't know," I answered, a thread of fear in my voice. "Keep hiding it. What else can I do?"

"Go to a doctor for starters!" Helen exclaimed.

"What can a doctor do? The doctor will just think I'm some crazy teen who isn't well supervised and my case will be turned back over to Child Protective Services. And then what? They'll pull me out of Huntington. I won't be able to live here at Thornfield anymore. There is only one thing I can do and that is keep it hidden and not tell a soul."

"You can't keep ignoring all the things that are messed up in your life, Jane! You can't ignore that tattoo. You can't ignore the dark things that are in this place. You can't ignore your past. For some reason that ghost contacted you and showed you the letters. And now your tattoo has expanded? What the hell!? Dark things are coming for you, Jane, and if that tattoo doesn't prove it, then I don't know what does."

"The only dark thing coming for me is midterm exams."

"You have to leave now!"

"Never going to happen."

I shook my head. "Go to sleep, Helen. I can't leave this place. I love it here. In my entire life, I've never had a real home. Here, I feel like I belong." I climbed into bed and closed my eyes. Helen climbed in beside me. "Please, can we just stop talking about this? I'm tired." It was true. I was exhausted. The events of the day, and the tattoo, had wiped me out. I closed my eyes and fell asleep quickly.

CH/\PTER 21

*Unha0py is he to whom the memories of
childhood bring only fear and sadness.*

~ H.P. Lovecraft

THE NEXT THING I KNEW Helen was shaking me
awake. She was shaking me so hard I probably had a bruise
on my arm. I sat up and she stopped shaking me, but I still
felt like my teeth were rattling.

"Do you hear that?" she asked.

"Hea⁻ what?"

"That!" she whispered.

I stopped and listened. All the usual old house noises
were present. The walls moaned a little. The plumbing
seemed to be rattling even when no one was using it. The
wind outside the windows hissed through the cracks in
the glass, making a phantom noise. Tree branches scraped
against the outside of the house. I didn't hear anything
disconcerting. I lay back down. I was exhausted and I just
wanted to sleep. I closed my eyes and was just drifting back
to sleep when I heard the laughter. I had almost become

accustomed to the ghostly laughing. I was so tired I didn't want to get out of bed, but Helen was pulling me from the mattress and I had no choice but to follow her into the hall.

"It's nothing," I said. "That happens all the time."

"Creepy laughter happens all the time? And you are okay with that?"

I didn't know what to say. Helen was as white as a sheet and she was trembling. Her eyes were wide with terror. I was afraid, too. I wasn't okay with anything, but the laughter had become part of my life, a bad recurring dream that I'd gotten used to in some weird way. I regarded it in the same manner Freud would regard a dream. It was a terror that had to be confronted in order to experience catharsis and move on. Unfortunately, every time I had tried to figure out the source of the laughter, it would fade away or become impossible to locate. I grabbed hold of Helen's hand and she leaned into me.

"What do we do now?" she asked. She was shaking so hard she made me shake, too. I had always imagined Helen would be brave in the face of this type of thing, but her courage was lost to the haunting laugh of a dead woman.

"We could investigate?" I offered.

Helen's laughter was hard and bitter. "Are you friggin' kidding me?"

I pulled Helen toward the door and opened it. The laughter was louder in the hall. The lights had flickered out, again, and the shadows had taken on strange shapes. Helen wouldn't budge, so I yanked on her hand and dragged her in the direction of the laughter. This time the laughter led us down the hall, past Edward's room. I followed it to the end of the hall where the back staircase led both up and down to the servants' quarters. The laughter came from below us. In the old days, I imagined every room would have been filled with a chambermaid or a butler, but now all those rooms were empty. Only dust and shadows filled the spaces that had once housed life. We pressed on, out the back door and into the gardens. The laughter filled the cool night air. It danced off the branches of trees and scared little birds into flight. Even bugs seemed to scurry away from the sound, but we pressed on. We followed it to a grassy place beneath the old tower room where I had found the sketch books. Our mouths dropped open when we saw her.

A girl's body lay in the grass like it had fallen from a great height. Helen froze beside me. She placed her hand on my arm. Her hand was so cold it was like ice. I shivered at her touch. The body lay in the grass and then it rose. It rose from the mud and greenery to stand up. The girl wore a long, red strapless gown and her long red hair was a tangled mess wrapped in red ribbons. I recognized her immediately. It was Edward's girlfriend from the picture. She smiled at us with a wicked grin, filled with a kind of twisted delight. Helen pulled me backward. She tugged me away from the grinning specter of the red-haired girl. We ran back to the house, as fast as our feet could carry us. If I had been trying out for track and field, I probably would have made the team, we were running that fast.

"You should leave this place," Helen whispered as we rushed into my room and locked the door behind us.

I shook my head. I was breathless from the running. My heart was pounding in my ears from the exertion. It was amazing how Helen was never breathless. There was never a hair out of place. She was always perfect.

"A haunted house is one thing," Helen said. "But you can't stay in this house, filled with hostile spirits. That ghost was angry."

"It might have just been sad. She looked like she died badly."

"Trust me on this," Helen said. "That is not a 'she.' That is an 'it.'"

"It just needs help," I said softly.

"I can't stay here," Helen said.

"You're afraid?" I was incredulous. Helen always seemed like the brave one before Thornfield.

"Come with me. We'll leave together," Helen implored.

"I have to stay," I said.

Helen shook her head. She tried to get me to leave with her, but I couldn't go. Helen tugged at my arm and pulled my shirt. She cried and begged. She promised me safety and friends and a normal college life, but I couldn't leave Thornfield. It was the closest thing to a home I'd ever had.

"I'm so sorry," Helen said. "I can't be here. This place doesn't like me. It won't let me stay. He won't let me stay." Helen looked up and I looked up. Helen's eyes were fixed on something above her, but there was nothing there. When I turned to face her again, she was gone. She'd left. She always did that. Would just pop in and out of my life. Granted, she did beg me to go with her. But I couldn't, I just couldn't leave. And I couldn't completely explain why. I just knew that I had to stay.

I plopped down on my bed. I couldn't sleep. I wasn't afraid anymore. The ghosts didn't scare me. I was upset because Helen and I had parted badly. I wished I could have gone with her, but my heart was bound to Thornfield Hall, for better or for worse. I opened the next letter and read it. I read on and on through the night. I read letter after letter. They went on for over two years. She implored him and he implored her. They wrote to each other in utter futility for all that time. They were like two lovers lost in the fog. Neither one of them could see each other, but their hearts ached for each other and my heart ached with each new letter I read. It seemed cruel that two people who loved each other so completely should be separated by their families. Their letters must have been intercepted and hidden from them. How sad. How tragic. Finally, Richard stopped writing and only Liliana's letters continued. I was careful with the next letter. It was tattered and so soiled I could barely make out the words on the page. My hands shook as I mounted the letter. I had to turn on an extra light to read it.

My Beloved,
I know now that you have abandoned me. Word has come home to me that you have wed another. My heart breaks and I wonder if you ever loved me at all. All my sisters are long since gone. They are wed with children

of their own and more on the way. There is only me left. I am left alone here, a lonely spinster waiting for a prince that will never come. I still wait for you. In the fog, I stand on the hill that looks out on your old home and dream of you. I find my heart turning dark. Where love once grew like a mighty oak there is now only shadow and fog and a seed of hatred so strong that even love couldn't dispel it. Oh, my beloved, if you had only answered one of my letters. If you had only whispered one kind word, I may have been able to stop the rage that has grown in my heart like a garden weed. It can't be stopped. You took my innocence and left me with nothing but a promise turned to dust. I am untouchable, now. No man will have me. I am too old and rumors of our affair have made me into something wicked and wanton.

I will never be a bride. There will be no white days for me. There will only be sorrow and sadness and death. Oh, my beloved, I have made a terrible mistake. The darkness came for me, my love. You were gone and the old god offered me his hand. I took it and now I am pregnant. My family has cast me out as a harlot and I am now alone in the ruins on Witching Hill. It is quiet here and I think the voices in my head may not be real. I can no longer tell. I like to imagine that the baby that grows in my belly is yours and that you will be home soon, but I know you will never come and even if you did, I gave myself to him. He waits for me even now. He promises me revenge

*and I shall have it, my love. Forgive me for what I
am about to do.*

*Forever Yours,
Liliana*

I set the letter down. Tears were streaming down my
face. I wasn't sure if it was Liliana or Helen who had made
me weep, but the tears wouldn't stop flowing. It was clear
Liliana had gone mad and they must have burned her for a
witch. It was a terrible story. I closed the book I had made
of the love letters and curled up beside it in the bed. I was
so tired, my eyelids pulled me down to sleep. I had three
letters left to read as I drifted off to sleep.

For the rest of the night, the ghosts at Thornfield Hall
were quiet and I dreamt. In my dream, I found myself wandering alone through the ruins on Witching Hill. It was
dark and there was a soft, steady rain that quickly soaked
through my clothing and left me shivering. I wandered
until I found a small room that still had the remnants of a
roof and I built a fire. I was so cold that even the fire did
nothing to warm me. Liliana was gone, but her old god
emerged to greet me.

Fear gripped me like it only can in dreams. In reality, I
can measure my emotion, choose my response. In the dream
I felt like death himself had my heart in his fist. The god
wasn't as I imagined. He wasn't hideous. He was handsome.
He was young and his face was kind. He had wild black hair
and skin that was dark with the texture of wood. His flesh

was covered in runes and his yellow eyes were luminous in the shadows. He smiled. The most shocking thing about him was the large ram's horns that grew from his black hair. He didn't wear a shirt and I could see he had the hooves of a goat. I don't know why I knew he was Liliana's old god. I just knew. I cowered in the corner, trying to hide myself in the shadows, but he saw me and there was no escape. I felt like I had felt when my foster mother locked me in that horrible room. I felt like the devil himself was smiling down on me and, somehow, I knew that the devil from my childhood and Liliana's god were the same man.

"Don't be afraid, sweet Jane," he said softly. "Your time is almost here, Jane of the Air."

I think I muttered something, but my voice was hollow and empty. It didn't carry through the cold night. "There is no need to be cold and alone. Come walk with me and I will show you the home you never had as a child." His voice was soft and soothing.

I pulled farther back into my corner. He was all smiles and soft words, but something in his eyes made my shaking even worse. He reached out for me and I screamed, and my screams carried with me into the morning. I sat up screaming. It was a beautiful day and the sunlight poured in through my window. I could hear the birds singing outside. It was warm and I was safe, but I could not stop my heart from racing and I couldn't help but feel that the horned man was still standing beside me, watching me.

Finally, my heart calmed and I fell back into my bed. I slept without dreams.

CHAPTER 22

"Nothing really known can continue to be acutely fascinating."

~ H.P. Lovecraft

I SLEPT IN TOO LATE and missed breakfast. The night before seemed like a haze and my head hurt in a way that I imagined someone who had stayed up late drinking might feel. I skulked out of bed. It was almost noon. It was a good thing I didn't have any classes that day. Three days weekends were my solace. Still though, I couldn't afford to fall behind in my studying. This haunted house thing was certainly interfering with my school work. I moved the books of letters, I had made, to the large desk. I was careful to put them in the desk drawer, away from the sunlight, to keep them safe. The sad tale they told lingered in my memory. In the shadow of that memory, was my fight with Helen and her reaction to the ghost. I phoned Helen, but she didn't answer her phone. I texted her and got in the shower. By the time I was out of the shower she still hadn't texted me back. I put on an old t-shirt and a pair of jean shorts and went outside.

I walked out into the gardens. I wasn't sure where I was going. I just wandered amongst the roses. A gentle breeze cut through the late summer heat carrying with it the scent of flowers and fresh cut grass. The last green of a dying summer was giving way to fall and soon the flowers would fade. I phoned Helen, again, but only the wind answered. A robin landed on the branch of a tree above me. It was a beautiful day. The leaves rustled in the breeze, singing a pastoral song. I turned into the breeze and walked back towards Thornfield. The day's beauty was lost to me. I had to find my friend. I would take my car and waste gas money if I had to.

I was so lost in my own thoughts, that Edward took me completely by surprise. He always seemed to be taking me by surprise. It was like I had forgotten I wasn't alone in Thornfield Hall.

"I hope you weren't wandering off," he said. "You're supposed to escort my grandmother to my party tonight."

I had forgotten about the party. "I have to go into town to find my friend," I protested. "I can't help you tonight."

"You made a commitment to me and to your job." Edward seemed so cold. He almost seemed like a different guy.

I offered Edward a weak smile and nodded. "Of course. I apologize."

"I'll expect you both in the ballroom at five."

Edward walked back toward Thornfield. I didn't have time to go to town to Helen's place. I had to get myself and Miss Adele ready for the evening. I took a deep breath. I couldn't imagine anything more loathsome than spending my evening at a party. I wanted to find Helen and tell her I was sorry for bringing her into something that terrified her so much. I wanted to apologize for not being more understanding, but the more I phoned and texted Helen, the more I knew she would never answer. Something had happened last night and I didn't really understand what it was.

The nurse had already dressed Miss Adele for the party by the time I arrived. I helped the nurse feed her some soup and give Miss Adele her medication. Adele was particularly coherent. I was grateful for that, at least. The old lady smiled as I walked her down the long hall to the ballroom. She hummed to herself. Right before we came to the ballroom, she turned and looked at me. She ran her hand through my long hair and looked at me so intently, I thought she must be looking through me.

"I'm so sorry, my dear," she said. "You are more haunted than even my grandson."

"What?" I asked

"Be careful," she said. "I have never seen spirits as devoted or as hellish as yours." She started humming, again, and then she opened the door to the ballroom and walked in. I followed behind her. I wanted to ask her what she'd meant, but I was overwhelmed by the room we walked into. The sound of music was dizzying and I wanted to cover my ears. I had never liked loud noises.

It was dazzling. It was like something from The Great Gatsby. The extra staff that Edward had hired had worked wonders. The room was filled with bistro tables and chairs;

the kind you see at a French restaurant. Loveseats had been strategically placed in more shadowy corners of the large ballroom so guests could have private places to talk. A long buffet table was against one wall and overloaded with various appetizers and finger foods. And a fully stocked bar, with three bartenders, was tending to a long line-up of thirsty party goers. The raised dance floor glimmered with disco balls and was crowded with couples dancing and gyrating to throbbing electronic tunes that were ever-changing and mixed by two DJs in the corner in a glass booth. Servers spun around the room at a dizzying speed, carrying trays of champagne and hors-d'oeuvres. Laughter and loud chatter mingled with the music. Some of the guests seemed drunk or like they were acting high. I never drank or used drugs, so I had no idea what they might be doing, but a haze of smoke hung in the room that made me feel lightheaded.

I was blinded by the noise and overwhelmed by the crowd. I had spent too much of my day hiding in the roses at the back of the estate. I hadn't seen the party coming and I wasn't prepared. Thornfield had come to life while I wept in the dark. I found myself longing for the ghosts and demons. I liked them better than the people that surrounded me in an almost manic kaleidoscope of noise and color. I wanted to run. I wanted to return to the roses but I assumed Edward would fire me if I ran and I knew Ms. Adele needed me.

The girls were wearing short, sparkly dresses that clung to their perfect figures. The guys were dressed in designer shirts and dress pants that showed off their athletic physiques. They all looked like celebrity reality TV stars. I looked down at the simple black dress and doc martins I was wearing. I had never felt more out of place. The black dress, aside from my white dress, which was kind of ruined from me falling in the dirt that night when I literally crashed into Edward, was the only good dress I owned. I'd found it at a little consignment shop back home. At the time, I was thrilled with the find. It was a simple cut with a square neck, sheer long sleeves and the hem fell just above my knees. It fit me perfectly, which was surprising because I always had trouble finding clothes that fit my long, narrow frame. I'd left my hair down, except for two braids on either side of my head that I'd clipped back with a black barrette. It was my favorite hairstyle, aside from the usual long braid I wore every day, and basically the quickest and easiest for me to do. But compared to the other girls at the party, I felt like a wren.

I slipped my arm through Miss Adele's and guided her to a sofa in the back of the room. I just wanted to hide and I sensed that it might be best for Miss Adele to hide, too. I tried my best to stay hidden in the smoke, but the constantly swirling lights made me dizzy and made it impossible to hide in a shadowy corner. I wanted to throw up. The music and light were too much for me and it would be too much for a frail old woman, too. Miss Adele and I sat down and she put her hand in mine. We watched the beautiful people move about the room like golden butterflies.

Edward stood in the center of the room. He was like the dark nexus of this glowing world. Girls stood around him, giggling and flirting. They were all so pretty. There were so many of them. Blondes, brunettes, red-heads, dressed in outfits that showed off their work-out toned bodies. One of the girls stood out from the others. Her long blond hair splashed over her shoulders like a golden halo, and her laughter rose above the music like it was the dominant force in the room. She only had eyes for Edward. She took his hand and led him off the dance floor and he followed like he was entranced. Seeing him with her made me light-headed. They looked perfect together. Her smile lit up the room and all eyes were on her, but he still didn't smile. He looked at her with his intense blue eyes, but, oddly, there was no smile on his face. I wondered why. Did he feel uncomfortable? Or maybe he didn't want to show his emotions in front of the party-goers? I couldn't help but remember the times he smiled at me. Did he actually, truly like me, or was it all a just a game that a rich and bored young man indulged in until his stunning girlfriend showed up?

Miss Adele looked at me. Her eyes were filled with tears. She looked very sad. And, inside, I felt the same way, too. It seemed like I had done my duty. We had sat at the party for as long as we could, but it was time to leave. Miss Adele was exhausted. I could see it in the way she slumped her shoulders. Edward hadn't even come up to us to say hello. Miss Adele was too old for this party, and I think I was, too.

I helped Miss Adele up and walked her back toward the door. We had almost made our escape when I felt Edward's hand on my shoulder. I stopped and both Miss Adele and I turned to face him. I looked up at him. The beautiful blonde was on his arm. Her hand was in his and her other hand was on his chest. She leaned up against him the way Miss Adele was leaning on me for strength. Her pale blue eyes were so light, they seemed like ice. Her skin was golden and smooth.

"Blanche," Edward said to the girl on his arm. "This is my grandmother Adele Rochester. Grandmother, this is Blanche I think she'll be next."

Miss Adele released my arm and walked toward the beautiful blonde. Miss Adele stood up straight and studied the girl. Adele seemed like a different woman. She seemed alert and studied Blanche as she would a prized pig.

"It's so nice to meet you," the girl gushed to Miss Adele. She giggled after she said the words. Blanche was so drunk she could barely stand.

Miss Adele studied the girl for a very long time. The music played on and the dancing continued. The world moved around us, but Miss Adele continued to stare at the golden blonde. The girl's smile faded and the giggle left her. She inched closer to Edward and wrapped her arms tightly around him. After what seemed like an eternity, Miss Adele nodded to Edward.

"Come, my dear," she said to me. "Time for bed."

Edward nodded back at his grandmother and didn't bother even sparing me a glance. Of course he wouldn't. Why would he? He had a gorgeous girl clinging to him. And I was just Plain Jane and only an employee in his household. Blanche was probably the daughter of some rich CEO or a well-connected Senator.

I took Miss Adele down the long hall toward her bedroom. The nurse had left for the night, so I helped Miss Adele get into her nightgown. I took off her wig and brushed her baby-fine gray hair. I helped her take her medication and I cleaned her dentures. Finally, I tucked her into bed. Miss Adele lay in her bed looking like someone at death's door. She seemed so tired.

"Did you enjoy the party?" I asked as Miss Adele drifted off to sleep.

"I hate parties," she said. "Edward hates parties, too. It is a shame he is a prisoner of this world. I would have loved to see him with a girl like you."

Her eyes shut and she drifted off to sleep. The valium I had given her per the nurse's instructions had wrapped her in its cocoon. I should have sat with her for a while, but I was tired, too. I felt my fatigue from the night before weighing heavily on me. The smoke at the party had left me disoriented and half-asleep. I hadn't slept much at all that week, but despite all of this I wasn't ready for bed. The music from the party floated up to my room. I called Helen again, but she still wasn't answering. I thought of reading the remaining letters, but the thought of Liliana drifting further and further into madness was too depressing for me. So, I wandered down to the library to find something to read. I wandered the stacks like I was a ghost myself. I wasn't sure what I wanted to read. Images of Edward and Blanche filled my mind and made it hard for me to focus. I'd pick up one book, get distracted, and move to the next. I couldn't find interest in anything.

"Did you like the party?" Edward took me completely by surprise, again. He always took me by surprise. I nearly jumped out of my skin.

"How do you keep sneaking up on me like that!" I exclaimed.

"It isn't hard. You always seem to be lost in thought, or with your nose in a book." He smiled and bent over and handed the book to me. As I took it from him, his hand brushed mine. The sensation sent goosebumps up and down my arm. I backed away from him.

"Parties aren't really my thing," I responded.

"But this was only the second party you've been to," he said with a quirk of his lips.

"Well, that's two not-so-great experiences, so I can safely say that I'm not a party person." I shrugged.

"You're reading, For Whom the Bell Tolls?"

"I was thinking about it. I'm not sure," I answered.

Edward took a step toward me. "I love Hemingway."

"He's not my favorite." I glanced down at the book. "I read The Old Man and the Sea, but I didn't like it that much."

"You should read this." He pointed to the book in my hand. "It is much better. I think you'd like it."

I looked at the book again. I tried to avoid Edward's piercing stare. I could still see him, in my mind, with his hand linked to Blanche's. They were clearly an 'it' couple. He was hers and she was his. I could still hear her laughter, dancing across the room like music. She was so pretty. I couldn't blame him for wanting to be with her. She was everything I wasn't.

I nodded. "I'll give it a try."

"You should come back to the party with me."

"No!" I exclaimed. I shook my head. "I can't do that. I'm not dressed right." I glanced down at the black leggings and t-shirt I had slipped on after I tended to Miss Adele. "And you need to be with all your friends."

"They're not my friends." His voice was cold and hard.

"They came all this way to a party at your house."

"When you're as rich as I am people follow you even if they despise you."

"Why bring them here if you hate them so much?" I asked.

"Because I wanted my grandmother to meet Blanche, and women like her are most comfortable traveling in packs."

I nodded as if I understood, but I didn't.

"We'll be leaving tomorrow," he said. "I have to get back to school, anyway. I was doing a directed study, but I have to check in with my advisor."

"I hope you have a good trip." I didn't even know he'd been in a directed study. I thought he had simply taken time off school or was starting next semester. I tried to swallow my emotion. I looked up and met his eyes. I clutched the book against my chest. I didn't want him to leave. He looked at me with his piercing blue eyes. Why did he always have to look at me like that? My lips trembled and I tried so hard not to cry. Is this how Liliana had felt when she said goodbye to Richard, only to never see him again?

Blanche sauntered into the room. She was wearing a tiny, gold bikini. She looked as out of place in the library as a polar bear in the Serengeti. She was still wearing sky-high heels and, in the bikini, she looked like a supermodel. She stumbled a little. She was clearly drunk or high. It didn't matter. She was so pretty she would have made Barbie feel insecure. Her figure and her skin were flawless. She wasn't marred by tattoos or scars. She giggled when she saw Edward and me standing together.

"What are you doing in here with the maid?" she asked.

"She's not the maid," Edward corrected her

"Whatever." Blanche giggled, again. I felt like I was back in high school. "She's just some dumpy servant girl. Don't you want to come join me in the hot tub?" Her voice became throaty. Her words were filled with innuendo. There was no mistaking what she was really offering him. He didn't even look at her. He just kept staring at me.

"Should I come say goodbye before I leave tomorrow?" he asked.

I looked down. I didn't want him to see the tears in my eyes. "Whatever you want," I whispered.

Blanche put her arms around Edward. She pressed herself up against him and pulled him to the door. She kissed his neck and whispered something in his ear.

He left with her and I was alone, once again, still clutching the copy of For Whom the Bell Tolls.

CHAPTER 23

Something like fear chilled me as I sat there in the small hours alone- I say alone, for one who sits by a sleeper is indeed alone; perhaps more alone than he can realize.

~ H.P. Lovecraft

SLEEP ELUDED ME THAT NIGHT. I couldn't get Edward out of my head, so I put Liliana into it. The last few letters were more like the ravings of a madwoman than letters to her long-lost beloved. They were barely legible and covered in filth. They were hardly letters at all. They looked like something you might see scrawled on the walls of a mental hospital, in some terrible horror movie.

> *Beloved,*
> *I am with you now. Do you feel me, I wonder? Does some part of your heart feel my heart beating inside you? Can you smell my hair even as you lie with your new bride? She is pretty and so young, too young. I doubt she has had her cycle for more than two moons.*

No matter. I envy her. She is so pure and so perfect. Her skin is white and her eyes are blue. I will take her eyes, my love. I will take them and use them to fashion a new bride for you; and your family and that bride will be called Hell; and she will follow you and all of your children until the end of time. I have already begun the ritual. My horned king, my sweet, dark lord tells me how to fashion Death from Mandrake root and the blood of the baby growing inside of me. I won't take much. I will take just enough blood to kill your bride. She will be dead soon and a new bride will come for you and she will kill you...

I can feel the baby moving inside of me. I will name her Jane. She will not be mine. She will be my god's. She will be a daughter of the old ones. I don't own any part of her. I have promised her to him. I wish you would sing to me now, my love. Sing to me like you used to. Tell me how you love my eyes. Tell me how milky white my skin is. I sing to you while you sleep. I creep up from the darkness below your Thornfield Hall, where I have taken up residence, and I sing to you. Tomorrow, I will take your bride's eyes, but tonight I will take your mother's head.

Forever Yours,
Liliana

I drew a deep breath and put the letter away. The room felt very cold and I pulled the covers up over me. The house was full of people, but I felt more alone than ever. Cocooned in fear, I had no choice but to keep reading. There was no other option. I couldn't leave my room and there would be no sleep for me tonight…

Beloved,

Tonight is the winter solstice; my dark god is king, tonight. He is the winter king and he loves me above all others, but I cannot love him for I will always be yours. I have fashioned you a new bride and you don't even see the difference. My dark lord brought me your sweet, soft bride and I cut out her eyes and tongue. I burnt her body and fashioned you a new bride out of her ashes, Jane's blood and filth. I gave your new bride with your old bride's eyes and tongue and, even though she is made of filth, her smile is still pretty. You still kiss her at night. You still love her. I killed your mother. You wept, but not enough. Is it incest now that you commit laying with your new bride? She has your mother's fingers. When she touches you, she touches you with your mother's hands.

Can you hear the voices, my love? Can you hear them? They tell me that it is almost time. My baby is almost ready to be born, but I have one last thing to do. One last curse before she comes. I have no soul left. All I have is hate and blood. When I am done, the very bricks of Thornfield will scream for centuries to come. All your children and your children's children will make love to blood and filth and death. You have forgotten me. You never loved me, but your children will remember my name.

Liliana

The next letter was caked in dried blood, but I read on. How could I stop?

Beloved,
This will be the last thing I write. This will be my last will and testament. Tonight, you and yours will see me burnt at the stake. I am a witch. I deserve to burn. I belong in hell with my brethren and my god. He will keep me safe there. There is no room in heaven for me. I gave birth to Jane, last night. I gave birth to her in the basement of Thornfield Hall. I screamed and labored alone in the dark. My blood stains the bricks there, now, and so does Jane's. We are part of this place, now. I held my sweet girl for a few hours. I kissed her head and then I carried her up to Witching Hill. I left her there, alone. My god will take her. She is his now as am I. It is strange. I thought she would be misshapen and hideous like my god. I thought she would have horns and goats' feet, but she was perfect. She was beautiful and quiet and sweet. I wanted to hold her forever. I wanted to let her suckle at my breast. I wanted to be her mother. For a moment, I remembered what real love felt like, again, and it hurt so terribly that the fire I face tonight seems like solace. Letting her go was

so much harder than letting you go. My arms ache for her now. I am sobbing. Can you taste my tears? They all think I am afraid of the fire, but I have nothing to fear there. I am afraid for her. I am afraid for her, alone on Witching Hill, with only my terrible lord to comfort her. What will he do with her? Where will he take her? This is all I ever need know of hell.

You hate me now. You hate me more than any man has ever hated any woman. All the love is gone and I must admit that if I could take it all back, I would. If I could be a maid, again, I would. I would never walk down the path that leads me to you. I would never let you take me in the green grass and leave me untouchable and forsaken. I would never wander the path to Witching Hill. I have earned your hate. The bride I fashioned for you tried to kill you in your sleep and you killed her. You held her and wept over her body and found that she carried your son and that he lived, but neither of them was real. You probably hold your son in your arms, now, and imagine him a gift from God. But your wife and son were not gifts from your God. They were gifts from my god, the god of the vast and infinite abyss. They are a gift from the old gods that call out to me. They are doors to a world filled with horror and wonder. Can you see a glimpse of that world when you hold your baby? Can you see that he is one of the old ones? You tasted my blood when you kissed your wife and the baby you hold in your arms is only mud. It has no soul. Now, the spell will seep into you *as you seeped into my life and created a soulless child. Now all your sons will follow in your path. They will marry young and all the women they love will die. Death will follow them like a lover. Their lips will be poison, as will yours. Forever, until the end of time, this shall be for Rochester men. Girl after girl will die in your arms and you will weep until you decide that love isn't worth it. Until you stop loving at all and you are empty and hollow and dead. Such is my curse. Such is your hell. You will die alone, knowing your sons will suffer as you suffered. Your sons will carry on forever, but they will all be soulless creatures made of my blood. There will never be hope or love. There will only be hate and loneliness that eats away at your soul until there is nothing left but rage. Until the very soul in you dies as my soul has died. Every woman they touch will wilt and die and if they don't touch a woman, the air they exhale will carry death with it. I have given you the gift of death, my love. Not death for you. Death for all those who come near you. Cruel and brutal death.*

I think they are coming for me. I wonder if I ever loved you, really. I wonder if such a thing as love can ever be real. Even still, if you came to me tonight and told me you loved me, I would end all this. I would end the curse and the blood. I would silence the chorus of demons and ghosts that have risen up to make your Thornfield their home. I would silence my own breaking heart. The night is long and dark. Forgive me.

The letter ended and I rested my head on my pillow. Liliana was right. The night is long and dark. I fell asleep dreaming of demon babies that bore my name and hoping that Edward wasn't sleeping in Blanche's arms. I wondered if I should have followed Helen and left Thornfield. But I couldn't imagine belonging anyplace else.

CHPTER 24

*"It might, too, have been the singular
cold that alienated me."*

~ .H.P. Lovecraft

EDWARD AND HIS FRIENDS LEFT in the morning.
He never did find me to say goodbye. It was for the best,
anyway. I stayed in my room all morning. With Edward
gone, Thornfield Hall grew quiet again. The extra servants
left and life went back to normal. I packed the letters away
and tried to forget about Liliana and Richard Rochester
and his descendant, Edward. My mind was quickly lost in
my school work. I spent my days mired in my classes and
studies, and my evenings were filled with all the books I
needed to read. I was determined to keep a 4.0 GPA, so I
buried myself in studying.

I took care of Miss Adele at night. I put her to bed
when I found her wandering the halls. I sat with her at
dinner, but Miss Adele changed after Edward left. She
grew distant and she stopped making sense. The nurse said
it was the Alzheimer's. She said that it would get worse with

time. I understood that. I had read enough to understand the dismal progression of dementia in an elderly woman nearing the end of her life, but Miss Adele seemed to be suffering from more than Alzheimer's. Her inner light had faded. It was like she was giving up on life.

Some evenings, after all my work was done, I would write long emails to Helen and send them off the next morning, at school, since the house had no Wi-Fi or Internet service. I hadn't been able to reach Helen since our fight. It was like she had vanished. I tried calling her. I'd even gone to her apartment, where she lived with her boyfriend Jake, but there was no one home every time I stopped by. It was weird. Like she'd completely disappeared.

The weeks passed quickly. School was everything I had hoped it would be. The people there were different than they had been in high school. They were focused and worked hard. It helped that all my advanced placement classes and testing had made it so I could skip all of my freshman level classes. I was in classes with people who were serious about their work. No one looked at me like I was a dork or a nerd when they found out I had the highest marks in all my classes. Instead, they came to me for help and respected me. It was an entirely new world and it felt good. Finally, my life was starting to feel good. In between classes, I would sit in front of Morton Hall, the biology building, and read my books in the grass. I would look up at the wondrous neo Gothic buildings and watch the clouds drift by. Sometimes, thoughts of Edward would drift through my mind like the clouds I would gaze at. I wondered if he was okay. How were his classes going? Did he still wish he was an English major? Was he still dating Blanche? On weekends, would he go off campus and head into Manhattan? Would he go to clubs and fancy restaurants with Blanche and her glamorous friends? I shook my head. It would make me crazy if I kept thinking about him. Not Liliana crazy, but still…

I was sitting on the grass going through my Chemistry notes, one warm October afternoon, when a young man came and sat down next to me. I recognized him from the pre-med group I had joined on campus. I hadn't talked to him, but I rarely talked to anyone, so this was nothing new. He was a little taller than me and slim with short, medium-brown hair and round wire-framed glasses. He reminded me of Harry Potter. He smiled at me and looked at the tattered copy of *For Whom the Bell Tolls* I had been dragging around with me since that night in the library with Edward.

"Doing a little light reading?" he asked.

I laughed and shook my head.

"We're in the same pre-med group. I'm Sinjun."

My eyes widened. "That's a cool name."

"It's my grandfather's name, very old English name; short for Saint John."

"Well, it's very unique.

"Thanks…

"Oh—I'm Jane," I said, realizing he was waiting for me to tell him my name.

He nodded and then shoved his hands in his pockets. "Hey, a few of us are putting together a trip to Haiti this summer. It's kind of an education-volunteer-help-the-poor-but-get-some-good-experience-too, kind of thing. Your name came up with one of the professors, I was talking with, as a promising pre-med student who might want to join us."

I was taken aback. I didn't think I had made that much of an impression on anyone. "Really?"

"Yeah. Dr. Blackwood has wonderful things to say about you. She thinks you're brilliant."

I blushed. "Wow."

I had two classes with Dr. Blackwood and they were notoriously the hardest classes in the pre-med curriculum. Dr. Blackwood had a reputation for making things hard for her students. I had put in my best effort and done very well on all my tests in her classes. I'd even gotten full credit on the essay questions, which was, apparently, unheard of. It hadn't been easy. I had stayed up late, studying until my eyes felt like they were going to fall out of my head; but I had done it.

"Anyhow," he continued. "I thought you might want to join us at some of the planning meetings for the trip."

"I would love to!" I said. "But I don't know if I'd have enough money to pay for airfare or accommodations or anything."

"We'll cross that bridge when we come to it. I just think you'd be a good addition to the team."

"Thanks," I said with a shy smile.

"The meeting is on Monday night at six. It's room 412 in Morton Hall... So, I'll see you there?"

I smiled again. "For sure."

Sinjun smiled back at me and, for a moment, he looked like he wanted to say something else, but he just said good-bye and stumbled away. I watched him leave. *Wow!* My hard work was actually being noticed.

I went to the medical mission meeting in Morton Hall that Monday night and then every Monday after that. I sat with Sinjun and two girls, named Mary and Sara, and we brainstormed ideas for the upcoming trip. Dr. Blackwood would join us with two doctors, who were supervising the mission, and they would oversee our plans. We planned fundraisers to collect donations, both money and stuff that we could bring to Haiti. Old glasses, vitamins, medicine. Over the following weeks, we managed to collect 60 boxes of Ibuprofen and 100 containers of prenatal vitamins.

Fall came and went quickly. Between my weekly meetings and my studies, I was so busy that I almost forgot about Helen and Edward. Almost. I had gotten used to the middle-of-the-night eerie laughter. I had gotten used to finding Miss Adele wandering the halls at night. I had gotten used to the expanded tattoo on my back.

I'd packed up Lillian's letters in a box and hid it at the back of my closet. I had no idea what I would do with them. Technically, they belonged to Edward. But I didn't have his cell number or even an email address. So, it wasn't like I could just text him or email him: *Hey I found a bunch of letters that I had no business reading, in the attic where I had no business snooping, written by a woman who was in love with one your ancestors. Oh, and she went insane and cursed your family, BTW, how's Blanche?* Yeah, like that would go over well.

No. For the time being, I would keep the box of letters in my closet and then wait to see what to do with them. I would keep waiting. That's what it felt like at Thornfield since Edward had left. There had been no more ghostly visitors. Whatever those strange spirits at Thornfield were doing, I had no idea. What do spirits do when they aren't popping up in hallways or attics ready to scare you? I also had no idea what they wanted from me. But it felt like they wanted something and I had no way of figuring that out.

CHPTER 25

We live on a placid island of ignorance in the midst of black seas of infinity, and it was not meant that we should voyage far.

~ H. P. Lovecraft

THE FIRST DAY OF DECEMBER was colder than usual. Snow flurries peppered the mountains in a blanket of white, and Thornfield Hall was so bitter I had to get up and check the space heaters in Miss Adele's room once a night to make sure she didn't catch a chill. I didn't dare use the fireplace for fear of another fire. I had just tucked Miss Adele in after I had found her wandering the library at 11:00 p.m. I went back to my room to finish my work on my final paper for my English class. I had finally invested in a laptop. I was making decent money and I needed it for my classes. I sat with my laptop in front of me and a mountain of books from the university library around me. My head was aching, but I wanted my paper to be perfect. My paper on French existentialists would be the last English paper I wrote. I wanted it to be magnificent.

I had read so many books about Albert Camus that I could quote him.

Thornfield Hall had been so quiet since that night with Helen, I had almost begun to believe the ghosts I had seen were products of our overactive imaginations. It all seemed so strange when you thought about it. I might as well have believed aliens had come to visit me. The only proof I had that it might have been more than a dream was the collection of letters. I should have given them to Mrs. Fairfax, but then I'd have to admit to her that I was in the attic, snooping. I certainly couldn't tell her a ghost told me to go up there. I knew the letters should be in a museum or in some Rochester family vault. I was surprised that all the rest of the stuff in the attic was just sitting there, collecting dust and mold. But that was none of my business. Besides, something about the letters held me enthralled. I liked to look at them in the evening and study them. Liliana's story ran through my head, over and over again, and I knew almost every word of each letter by heart. I was doodling the horned man, from my dream, in the margins of my notebook late one night and my head began to throb.

I took my glasses off and set them down on the night-stand and rested my eyes for a moment. When I put them back on, the white lady was standing right in front of my bed. I jumped backward and my books and papers flew off the bed. I screamed and then put my hand over my mouth to muffle the noise. I had almost begun to believe that the ghosts had been my imagination.

"Run!" the white lady whispered.

I sat, frozen in place. My heart pounded in my ears like a big bass drum. I couldn't find the courage to breathe let alone run.

"Run!" the ghost said again.

Slowly, fear melted into curiosity. My hand came down from my mouth and I studied the spectral visitor in front of me. She was diaphanous and beautiful. She was dressed in a simple white gown. Her long, dark brown hair spilled down her back like a waterfall. She seemed sad.

"Are you Liliana?" I asked.

The ghost nodded. "He's coming," she said, fading in and out. "You need to leave this place." Her voice floated around me, swirling around my head. "Leave now. Fight your fate. Run." For a minute, I thought I must have been suffering from sleep deprivation. Too much Red Bull and too much Camus had addled my brain and turned me into a psych case. I rubbed my eyes and Liliana was gone. It had all been a dream.

Then the laughter started. It began far away and it crept up the hall. As it grew closer to me, it became louder and louder, until I had to put my hands over my ears to stop it from driving me crazy. I crawled under the covers and pulled them up to my chin. The lights flickered off, leaving me in the dark. I screamed. I didn't do anything to muffle my scream. I just screamed. My laptop shut down and complete darkness consumed the room. The laughter became so loud that I couldn't shut it out.

"Go away!" I shrieked. I yelled until I went hoarse. The laughter finally faded and the lights turned on. My laptop flickered to life, but all my work was lost. My fear dissipated, replaced by something worse than fear, as I realized I hadn't backed up my term paper. The ghost suddenly seemed like a very small thing compared to my lost term paper. I yelled again and, this time, I added a couple of curse words to my cry. I almost wished the ghost had just killed me.

I said another curse word that was completely out of character for me just before I heard Miss Adele shriek. I jumped out of bed and ran into her room. She was sitting up.

"Edward!" she yelled. "Edward! Where are you, my love?"

"Edward's gone back to Yale," I said as I started to brew the tea I would use to give her valium.

"No, no," she muttered. "He's still here. I can see him. He wants it to end. He says it should end." She turned and spoke to the corner. "Forgive me, Edward. Forgive me. I knew you never loved me. I knew. I will fix it. I will end it!"

I sat down next to Miss Adele. I stroked her back and handed her the tea. "It will be okay," I said in my most comforting voice. "Edward loves you. He's away at college."

"Please, Edward!" she continued. Her eyes were wide with horror. "Please! I promise. I promise I will fix it. I will bring him home and I will fix it and I won't care if it all burns. I promise."

"Drink your tea," I told her as I put the teacup to her lips. She stopped her rant long enough to drink the tea and then she got out of her bed. I didn't want to stop her. I was afraid I would hurt her. She hadn't been eating and she had grown so thin and so frail I thought I would crush her bones if I moved her against her will.

She walked over to the corner and stared into the nothing that lived there. She seemed to be leaning against some imaginary form. She grew quiet. "I will do it," she whispered. "I will stop everything. I will release him. It will all burn, my beloved. It will all burn. I promise you the door will stay closed."

I walked up to her and gently put my hand on her arm. "It's all right," I said as soothingly as I could.

Miss Adele turned around and the most monstrous expression covered her face. She slapped me and I flinched. I wasn't hurt, but I was shocked. "Get out!!! Get out!!! You can't be here. You are the devil! Don't you think I see you! Don't you think I see you! I see your father. I see what you will do! You are the devil! You are hellspawn!"

I backed away, holding my cheek. Miss Adele stopped screaming and wandered into the corner. I let her stand in her corner until her muttering became inaudible, and then I slowly guided her back to her bed. I tucked her in and stroked her hair until she fell back to sleep. I would have to talk to Mrs. Fairfax in the morning. I wasn't qualified for this level of care.

I returned to my room and became so absorbed in rewriting my term paper that the ghosts and wailing old ladies faded from my mind.

CHAPTER 26

*I have looked upon all the universe has
to hold of horror, and even the skies
of spring and flowers of summer must
ever afterward be poison to me.*

~ H.P. Lovecraft

THE NEXT MORNING CAME AND I hadn't slept, at all. I had managed to rewrite most of my paper using my notes, but I knew it was going to be a long day. I stopped going down for breakfast with the rest of the staff. I had too much work to do and no time to linger over a leisurely breakfast, but I went to breakfast that morning and caught up to Mrs. Fairfax afterward. She smiled at me with her usual maternal grin.

"What can I do for you, Miss Marsh?" she asked pleasantly.

"I need to talk to you about Miss Adele," I said. "Her nightly wanderings have become more frequent and last night she was ranting gibberish for a while. I was afraid she might hurt herself."

"Oh dear," Mrs. Fairfax said.

"I love working here, Mrs. Fairfax. I love Thornfield Hall and you've been so kind to me and the pay is beyond generous, but I don't know if I'm qualified to meet Miss Adele's needs anymore. I'm not a medical professional and I wouldn't have known how to stop Miss Adele if she had taken it in her mind to really hurt herself last night."

"Miss Adele adores you," Mrs. Fairfax said. "She would be miserable if you left and you've gone above and beyond the call of duty, again and again, with her. I can't imagine anyone we could hire who would do better than you. Not to mention the fact that we've never been able to keep a night staff member for more than a month. Please, Jane, don't leave us. You have been a Godsend for Miss Adele and you've eased my worries on the matter."

"I couldn't live with myself if something happened to Miss Adele while she was under my care," I said passionately.

"Jane, I assure you, there is no one else more qualified than you. Even the nurses can't keep up with Miss Adele the way you do. She runs away from them. They find her in the attic and the gardens. I've had two nurses quit in the last month. They all say she needs to be in a nursing home. You are brilliant with Miss Adele. She listens to you. You calm her down. Please stay. I will pay you more. I can pay you anything you want. I will triple your pay. Edward won't mind. He thought all the other girls were twits and he hasn't had a bad thing to say about you."

"Have you ever thought that she would be better off in a nursing home?" I said firmly. I was being far more forward than I usually would be, but last night had convinced me that Miss Adele needed more intensive care. I was worried, and my worry overwhelmed my usual shyness.

"That's impossible," Mrs. Fairfax said with an unusual harshness.

"But—" I began to protest.

Mrs. Fairfax cut me off. "I said that is impossible. Will you stay on?"

"O-of course," I said with a smile. "I just wanted to do the best I could for Miss Adele."

"That is why I could never replace you. Your paycheck will be triple what it was last week," Mrs. Fairfax said with a sweet smile. "Now, if you'll excuse me, I have to go call Edward."

"Edward?" I asked. The mere mention of his name made my heart pound.

"Yes,' she said. "Miss Adele is insisting he come home. He may not come, but I must relay her message."

"Good luck," I said as I turned to leave. I didn't want Mrs. Fairfax to see the hopeful smile that had spread out over my face. Edward might be coming back. I could hardly breathe. I would see him again. I knew he was dating Blanche. I had no unrealistic expectations, but it didn't matter. It would be wonderful just to see him again.

To be continued…

ABOUT THE AUTHOR

Jessica Penot is a therapist and a mom. She lives in Huntsville, Alabama with her children, husband, dogs, cats, and other strange creatures. When she's not writing, she's probably exploring a haunted house somewhere with her husband and kids.

Jessica's latest writing project is a YA/NA paranormal series called the *Tattooed Girl Series* inspired by Charlotte Brontë's beloved classic novel, *Jane Eyre*.

The Tattooed Girl Series includes the following books:
Jane of Air (Book 1)
Jane of Fire (Book 2)
Jane of Water (Book 3)
Jane of Earth (Book 4)
Jane of Darkness (Book 5)
Jane of Light (Book 6)

You can learn more about Jessica at www.jessicapenot.com. Sign up for Jessica's *Scary Girl Newsletter* and follow her on Facebook, Instagram, Twitter and Tumblr .